WHATEVER SHE WAS, SHE WAS BEAUTIFUL

More than beautiful, thought Dr. Leif Barker, as he ran his hands across her spectacular body on the operating table. He was afraid . . .

The X-ray had indicated something very strange. He had to find out what the alien objects in Halla Danto's body were. And he had to work fast. Before *Timestop!*

A WOMAN A DAY

Philip José Farmer

Award-winning author of

RIVERWORLD

Berkley Books by Philip José Farmer

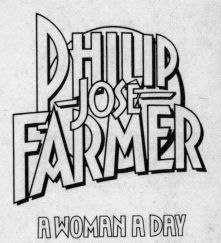

A WOMAN A DAY

BERKLEY BOOKS, NEW YORK

This Berkley book contains the complete
text of the original edition.
It has been completely reset in a type face
designed for easy reading, and was printed
from new film.

A WOMAN A DAY

A Berkley Book/published by arrangement with
the author

PRINTING HISTORY
Lancer Books edition published 1968
Berkley edition / July 1980

ISBN: 0-425-04526-9

A BERKLEY BOOK® TM 757,375
PRINTED IN THE UNITED STATES OF AMERICA

Chapter 1

DOCTOR LEIF BARKER pulled the woman to him. She did not resist; she had not come to him to resist. Not at this point. Her actual intention, as he knew, was to yield so far and then scream until the men who were undoubtedly waiting nearby would burst in and arrest him. Or pretend to arrest him.

The woman looked up at him, her rouged lips half-open. She said, "Do you think this is real?"

"It's factual," said Lief, and then his lips closed over hers. She responded wildly—a little too wildly, for he knew that she was acting. Overacting. Or was she? Perhaps she enjoyed her job more than she would have wanted her superiors to know.

He reached up with his right hand. Before she knew what he was doing, he seized the ruffled collar around her neck and ripped open the back of her dress.

Her eyes opened, and she tried to pull away, to say something, but he kept his mouth over hers. Before she could move she was stripped to the waist. Then he released her, but his right hand was open, ready to chop against the side of her neck if she tried to scream.

However, she seemed stunned by the rapidity with which the seduction was taking place. And, perhaps, she had not been in the business so long that she was cynical about a lamech-wearer. Perhaps her conditioning still held, telling her that a man in Leif Barker's position was irreproachable. Perhaps.

Whatever she thought, she was lovely. Whoever had sent her had chosen a woman who would make resistance difficult. She was a tall slim blonde with the body of a fully developed woman but a face that still suggested the innocent child. A passionate child, yes, but still a child. However, exposed as she now was, the large, firm breasts robbed her of the immature appearance and made it easier for Leif to do as he had planned.

Her hands had been hanging by her side; now, aware of his gaze upon her breasts, she put up her hands to hide them. He laughed.

"What is the matter?" he said. "Have you now decided that you do not want me to become your lover? That you have not always admired me from afar and that it was a mistake to come here and give yourself to me? That you have decided not to go against the teachings of the Sturch?"

"No," she said, her voice trembling. "I—I just did not expect that—that . . ."

"That things would go so fast you might actually have to go through with it before your friends could get here?" he said, still smiling.

She turned pale. She opened her mouth to say something, but the paralyzed throat refused to allow the words to come.

"It's a sign of the times," he said.

"What is a sign?" she managed to say.

"Once," he said, "a man who wore the lamech—" he touched the large golden Hebrew L which he wore pinned to his shirtfront—"was regarded as above temptation. Being above temptation, he was also above suspicion. There were no attempts by the Uzzites to make him prove that his conduct was based on reality, by trying to seduce him into immorality. But these are degenerate times, and now no man is above suspicion."

He paused and said harshly, "Tell me, did Candleman send you?"

She flinched; he knew that he had struck the truth. So—his own superiors in the Cold War Corps were not testing him. He was being trapped by Candleman, the chief of the Uzzites, the secret police of the Haijac Union.

"How many men are waiting?" he said.

She did not reply, so he took her by the hands and pulled them away hard, exposing her breasts. She turned her head away so she would not have to look him in the eye, and the paleness of her skin was replaced by a blush that spread from the hips upwards.

"You won't tell me?" he said. "It doesn't matter. Look!"

He released her and went to the wall, pressing against a section of it. Instantly, a square just above his hand flickered and became a screen, and the interior of the waiting room in the penthouse was revealed. Three men were slumped unconscious on the floor. They wore the black uniforms of the Uzzite.

"As a lamech-wearer, I have many privileges," he said. "One of them is the right to take precautions against the violation of my person. So I have this. I press a button, and an anesthetic is released into the waiting-room."

"But the gas circuits were supposed to—" She stopped.

"Have been de-energized by one of your friends?"

he said. "They probably were. But I'm not such a fool that I didn't install a duplicate circuit—one even Candleman wouldn't know about."

She was pulling at the front of her dress again, her blue eyes wide with fear.

"Why are you telling me this?" she said. By her question he knew she thought he was going to kill her.

"Because you are going to continue to work for Candleman," he said. "And you are also going to be working for me. But your real loyalty will be to me. You'll be afraid to expose me to him."

"What do you mean?" she gasped.

He approached her slowly, reaching out for her dress again.

"You know Candleman. He will not tolerate unreal sexual conduct, even on the part of his agents. I know that you were supposed to get me aroused and then call your friends. Candleman, who is so moral that he doesn't mind killing a man or trying to tempt a lamech-wearer, would not tolerate one of his girls actually going through with the act."

"You don't mean . . . ?"

"Yes, of course. I'll have you now. You'll be in no position to betray me to Candleman. Besides, you're lovely, and I've not had a woman for a month now."

"Your wife?" she said, stepping back.

He laughed and said, "My wife and I have never even kissed each other."

She continued retreating until she felt the cold wall against her bare back. Then, suddenly, she fell on her knees before him.

"For the love of the Forerunner!" she begged. "Do not do this! I will be forever lost!"

For a moment, Lief actually thought of allowing her to go. Then he told himself that would be the act of a fool. If he did not go through with this, he would have to kill her to prevent her from accusing him to

Candleman. He certainly did not want to do that. Moreover, she was lovely.

"Ingrid, my dear," he said, "I don't think that you will find this as distasteful as you think."

"Please don't!" she said, her voice breaking. "I had to do this! Candleman would have had my father put in H if I did not!"

He hesitated. Perhaps her story was true. But he doubted it. Candleman would not trust an agent who did not have the same fanaticism as himself.

"You are lying," Leif said. "And even if you aren't, I want you."

He put his hands under her armpits and raised her. Within five minutes she had quit struggling, and in another minute she was acting as wildly as before Leif tore her dress. This time Leif was certain that she was not pretending.

Chapter 2

THE TRANSPARENT QB cube upon the wall flicked. The miniature storm inside it flung itself about like a caged beast. Clouds roiled; lightning flashed.

Abruptly, chaos became order. The QB cracked and sputtered, and figures appeared in it. One of them was a man seated behind a desk. For a few seconds, the scene shimmered. Then, as if the essence of the tiny man had decided to become existence, the figure became as hard and sharp-edged as fact itself.

The cube held the projection of a government gandy studio. The desk and the reporter behind it and the wall-sized portrait of Isaac Sigmen behind him were real as life, if only a sixth as large.

Dr. Leif Barker, sipping his breakfast coffee in his penthouse atop the Rigorous Mercy Hospital, sleepily watched his QB. The instrument was daily becoming less efficient. He could call in the overworked techs. If they could requisition the needed materials—a big if—they could have the QB working at ninety percent efficiency. But the shoddy materials they would get could not keep it from slipping back to its normal seventy-eight per cent.

No, there was no use calling the techs. These breakdowns were signs of the times.

He sipped the skin-searing liquid.

Very good signs of the times, too.

Leif liked them, for he was their prime mover, the spider who squatted in the center of the web and strummed the strands from time to time.

" . . . and it may or may not be real that Timestop will occur within a year," the gandyman was honking. "But we're authorized to say that events of the last six months seem to point to such a possibility. You all know what we're referring to, the strange signs and portents that have been so numerous recently."

Sleepily, Leif smiled. Yes, the Haijac Union's government had itself started rumors of Timestop, the prophesied day when Sigmen would return from his travels through past and future to the present. That day could see the destruction of his enemies and the rewarding of his faithful. Every follower of reality would be given a universe of his own to play with; he'd have no more authority above him, no guardian angels to check on his every move.

The Haijac government had itself created events designed to take the citizens' minds from long work and short pay. But the Cold War Corps of the Free State of March had caught the ball and was rolling it downhill, where it was causing an avalanche. They had a plan to make the rank-and-file Jack a fervent believer in the close arrival of Sigmen, the Forerunner.

And when the citizenry was expecting Timestop every day, then watch out! For they'd not only get one Forerunner, they'd get a . . . and he drifted off into thoughts of the frantic efforts of the Jack bureaucracy to dam the flood they themselves had started. There would be nothing more upsetting, more revolutionary, than a man who sees his expected millenium proved to be a fraud.

That—plus one other important movement Leif was closely connected with—might wreck an empire.

Halfway through his second cup, the buzzer sounded. Annoyed, he flicked the toggle. Immediately the scene in the cube dissolved. The mist that replaced it flickered, was shot with quartz that ran the spectrum, and then cleared to a not-quite focus. The figure of his secretary was revealed, sitting behind her desk ten stories down.

Revealed, thought Leif Barker, wasn't the right word. Not when a thick, highnecked, floor-length dress covered her presumed figure. The virtues stamped upon her wax-like character by the Sturch had not been smoothed out in rubbing against her boss. Rachel was a *real* girl. You'd not catch her in any behavior that might possibly lead to a pseudo-future. She was *real*.

He stared at her. She blushed.

"Yes?" He felt like growling, but he smiled instead. If he could break his face into the desired joviality, he'd be all right the rest of the morning.

"Dr. Barker, there's a Zack Roe who insists he's to see you."

Leif didn't permit his smile to change.

"His appointment is not until ten this morning. Tell him he's made a mistake."

Another small figure entered the cube and looked at the little glass box upon Rachel's desk. Zack Roe was a tall and stooped man with grey hair and the OD's of a laborer. He spoke Icelandic with a slight Siberian accent.

He held his hat in his hand, and ducked his head as he said, "Please, Doctor. I know I'm not here at the right time. But I forgot that today I start my purifications rites."

"What're you doing here?"

"I thought maybe you could give me my tests now. That way we'd both be satisfied. I know these tests are important, doctor."

He ended with a giggle and a bulging of his blue eyes.

Leif sighed and said, "Shib, I'll be right down. Rachel, tell Sigur to turn on the eegie, will you, please?"

Rachel said she would. Leif flicked the screen off, drank his coffee, thought it scalded his tongue, and rapidly munched his seaham and eggs. Roe had given the key words—*that way* they meant that Leif was to contact him as fast as possible.

Something big was up. Otherwise, Zack would never have broken the pattern of his ways and thus given his gapt a reason for investigating him. Fortunately, he had a good excuse. Purification rites came ahead of everything else, and his role as a stupid shovelman would fit it with his apparent forgetfulness.

Leif strode through several rooms, furnished quite well for these drab and dismal days, and walked toward the elevator. His collie, Danger, leaped for him and was quite offended when his master only scratched his ears as he went by.

"Later," said Leif, pressing the button that would take the car down to the eegie rooms.

There was no reason to be alarmed at the unusual pattern of events, but he felt uneasy. The Plan had been going well—almost too well. But he must not allow an expression of anxiety to cross his face. What had he, a lamech-wearer, to fear? Smiling, he dismissed the thought from his mind and returned to the hospital routine.

He yearned for another coffee. And yawned. Yearn and yawn. He smiled to himself. He seemed to be doing a lot of both lately—though last night had taken the edge of the yearn.

The door opened. He walked into Rachel's office.

She said, "Good morning, doctor."

He said, "Forerunner bless you. Any important mail?"

He didn't want to give the impression of haste. She might wonder about concern over a nonentity like Zack.

She said, "No letters, *abba*."

"Don't call me father," he said. "I'm only ten years older than you."

"I respect you as a father," she said, eyes downcast.

He lifted her chin and kissed her on the mouth. "Here's a fatherly buss. You get one every time you call me *abba*."

He chuckled and said, "And as a reward for *not* doing so, you also get one every time you *don't* call me father."

"Doctor Barker! You mustn't do that!" Her cheeks were flaming.

He grinned at her and said, "I'm taking unfair advantage of you because I'm a lamech-wearer. On the other hand, what's the use of being one, if you can't take advantage of it?"

Her mouth hung open. Leif resisted the temptation to close it with another kiss. Though beautiful, she was more cold candy than warm flesh. The man who broke down her defenses would find that he'd have done better to spend his time elsewhere. She wouldn't be good business; the overhead would be large and the assets frozen.

Ah, well, she was a human being and not responsible for all of what she was. He stepped into the elevator, turned, waved Rachael a cheery good-bye, and dismissed her from his mind. Something big was brewing; probably his life was involved.

Chapter 3

WHEN LEIF ENTERED the eegie room, he found that Sigur had seated Zack Roe and had placed the tantalum helmet over the grey head.

Zack exposed his buckteeth in a smile and said, "Sigmen love you, doctor."

"A real future to you," replied Leif. He nodded, and Sigur pushed a button. The kymograph beneath the eegie machine began turning. Accompanying it was a beep-beep noise which, as part of the experiment, was supposed to distract the subject. The experiment was, ostensibly, an attempt to correlate the brainwave pattern of the subject with his vocalization. For some time Leif had been spending an hour a day on this project to read a man's mind through electronic means.

Actually, he had been doing just that for the past two years. The lower half of the so-called electroencephalograph was what it was supposed to be. It recorded the subject's brainwaves on a kymograph. But the upper half of the eegie was the machine which had been smuggled into Leif's hands by the

Cold War Corps. It did what the other was eventually intended to do. It could "read" a man's mind. And at this very moment it was detecting and amplifying Zack Roe's thoughts and transmitting them through the supposedly meaningless beeps.

"I'll ask the usual number of test questions," said Leif. "Answer 'yes' or 'no.' I don't care whether or not you tell me the truth now. Later, I want you to indicate the true answers. Got it?"

"Yah," drawled Zack. "I ain't as dumb as you think, doc. We done that before, din't we?"

Leif glanced at Sigur. He was standing by the kymo, his back to them, watching the stylos inking the alpha, beta, gamma, kappa and eta waves. The beeping continued; Sigur paid no attention to the noise.

"When were you born, Zack?"

"The third of Fertility, 190 A.R.," Zack said.

Leif checked that in his note book, then he winked at Zack.

"Answer the same question in English, Zack. We want to check any difference in the waves effected by using different tongues."

Zack complied.

At the same time, the beeps changed their pattern. Leif's ear picked it up at once.

What took you so long, Leif? This is hot. You should have come running. Shib. Here's the message. Halla Dannto, the wife of the Archurielite, was hurt at 7300 in an auto collision. She was taken to this hospital. You're to get to her fast. Fast! Get the doctor on-call off the case and call Ava.

If Halla Dannto is dead, cremate her body without delay. Don't let anybody besides Ava know you're burning it. Then go back to her room and act as if she's still alive.

Get this! Don't mention Halla's death to the woman who'll take her place.

She'll be wearing an old-fashioned street veil when she comes in. Ask no questions. Accept her as the real Halla Dannto. Got it?

As if he were thinking of something, Leif nodded his head.

He said, "Now, Zack, next question."

Rachel rushed into the room.

"Doctor Barker!" she said breathlessly. "Doctor Trausti just called me and gave me a message for you. Your QB didn't seem to be working, so I brought it myself. You're to come down to room 113 at once. The wife of Archurielite Dannto has just been brought in, badly injured. Trausti wants you to take over."

Leif raised his eyebrows.

"Can't he handle it?"

"I suppose he thinks she's too important for him. Besides, she might die."

"And he wants me to take the responsibility for that?" said Leif, smiling. "Tell him I'll be right down. And, Rachel, get hold of my wife. Demand she drop everything, even if it's a baby, and get down to 113. Shib?"

He turned.

"Sigur, that cancels the experiments for the rest of the day. Tell the other subjects they can leave now."

He strode from the room. Outside, he collided with a man who was standing just in front of the door. The fellow staggered backwards; Leif had a fleeting impression that the impact had not been that hard, that the man was exaggerating a little.

"Pardon me," he said, and he went to pass on. A strong hand upon his arm stopped him.

The stranger coughed and then said, "Doctor Barker?" His voice was high and had a slightly foreign accent.

"I'm in a hurry. See you later," said Leif.

He absorbed the man with a glance. He liked to

know who the people were around him, what they looked like, and what they were doing. Afterwards, he could give you the essential details.

Leif was struck. There was something *strange*, almost artificial about him. He was short and stocky and had a very light skin and hair and light blue eyes. The lobeless ears were large. The nose was a contradiction with its broad flaring nostrils and high arch. The lips were thick.

"What's your name?" demanded Leif.

The fellow coughed.

"We . . . I mean I'm Jim Crew."

Leif caught the "we" and looked at the others sitting in the waiting room. A man and two women, all young, their faces looking enough like Jim Crew to make them his brothers and sisters.

"You're all here for the eegies?" he asked.

"No, *abba*," said Jim Crew. He looked at the others. Two of them closed their eyes. Their eyelashes were long and thick as spider's legs. Tension suddenly pulled up the slack in the air. Leif felt as if there were invisible threads drawing around him.

"What do you want?" he asked.

"*Abba*," said Jim Crew, "we've come to you because you're the only man in Paris who can help us."

One of the woman rose to her feet. Her face leaped at Leif with a blonde and savage beauty. At the same time, her expression was strangely abstracted. "If you could picture flesh as such a thing, it was like a cubist painting of an ancient saint.

"Our child is dying," she crooned, low and throaty. Her thick lips trembled, slurring the words.

She held her hand out. Jim Crew took it. They said, together, "Our child has been struck by the same auto that killed Halla Dannto."

The third woman, still sitting on the divan, her eyes closed, moaned, "Our child is dying. Her skull is cracked open, and there is a splinter of bone pressing upon her brain.''

The other man suddenly laughed. Contrasted with the evident distress of the others, the laugh was shocking. Leif winced.

"It doesn't matter," the man said. "In one way, no. In another, yes. But if you don't come quick, our child will be dead.''

Leif felt as if he were in a dream. He was impatient to get to Mrs. Dannto's room. Yet, he couldn't leave.

"What do you know about Mrs. Dannto?" he said. "How do you know she's dead?"

"We know," said Jim Crew. "We also know she lives again.''

"I have to go to Mrs. Dannto," said Leif. "I'm sorry about your child, and I'll do all I can for her as soon as possible. What room is she in?"

"She's not here," replied the standing woman. She opened her eyes. Bright and light blue, they shone with a glow that did not come from the light-panels.

"Our child is in a room deep under the city."

"What is this all about?" barked Leif. "Tell me quickly. I've little time for nonsense.''

The man on the divan said, "Nonsense such as we mean—" he waved his hand to take in the two women and Jim Crew—"is the only real sense.''

Jim Crew smiled with big teeth and sad lips.

"She was struck by the auto that crashed into Halla Dannto's car. We did not bring her here because that would have meant her death—and ours.''

The savage beauty moaned, "And our child knew that she might be crushed, and that you might have to come to her and save her.''

"I'm intrigued," said Leif in a deep voice, the cords on his muscular neck standing out. "But I don't know what you're talking about. And I'm beginning to wonder why you think I wouldn't call the Uzzites. You're evidently a case for them."

"You wouldn't do that," said Jim Crew.

"You couldn't," said the beauty. "We know. Our child knew."

"You'll come to the sewers," said the second woman.

"Like H I will," said Leif. "If you want me to operate on your child, bring her here."

He strode away, brushing past Jim Crew.

As he went through the door, he halted in mid-stride, almost as if the air had jelled around him.

Out of the air had come an unsound, a voice that had no syllables borne on no air waves, yet unmistakably made itself heard.

"Quo vadis?"

He turned around.

"What are you doing?"

Jim Crew said, "Don't feel violated, Dr. Baker. We did it so you'd know we're not . . . crackpots."

"Nor," added the savage beauty, "people to be slighted."

She looked at him, and he was suddenly filled with a grief that he could contain only by the most violent effort.

He didn't like it, and his face must have shown it, for in the next second it was gone, leaving him wondering if he had not been imagining it.

The man on the divan laughed loudly again. And Leif felt like laughing back.

He gripped the side of the door and squeezed. With the feel of strength came a summoning of rejection. They were looking at him now, all eight eyes blue with a glare that seemed to be a focus of something shining from inside them: a single light rayed through four pairs of peep-holes. He wouldn't soak any of that light up! He was a mirror, reflecting it back at them, unabsorbed! Master of himself, the way he wanted it, the way he *had* to have it.

"I truly would like to come," he said. "But if you know so much, you know I can't."

"Ah," breathed Jim Crew through his high-bridged, Gothic nostriled nose, "but you can. Halla Dannto is dead. You can do her no good."

He felt as if the floor were slipping away from him. He was sure there should be only three who knew she had died; the intern, Zack and himself. And he and Zack weren't sure.

But he didn't have time to investigate them. Zack had been too insistent on the speed with which he got to room 113 and the secrecy he kept thereafter. Big, dark things, were moving in the background, and he had no time to stop and talk.

He slammed the door and walked across the room to the QB. He dialed Rachel. The transparent cube projecting from the wall flickered into a miniature of her office. And at once began flickering again.

"Rachel," he said, "did you get hold of Mrs. Barker?"

"Yes, sir. She's coming right now."

He twisted the dial and started to walk away when Rachel's voice called. "Dr. Barker. Wait! Rek calling."

He turned and dialed her in again. This time her image came in clearly.

"I'll tune you in with Archurielite Dannto," she said. He saw her press some buttons on her desk, and then her office faded away. It was replaced by another, a far larger and more luxuriously furnished office. The desk was huge and dwarfed the man standing behind it. Absalom Dannto was a big man with enormous shoulders, a mountainous paunch, and two chins, the lower of which quivered like the bag of a frightened cow. Leif smiled at the thought and then wiped it off, for the Archurielite was not a man to be trifled with.

Dannto's voice boomed through lips distinguished by their absence. "Barker? I've just been told my wife was in an accident and that she's in your hospital. Is she hurt badly?"

Leif was surprised. The man seemed genuinely concerned.

"No, *abba*. I've just been told. You interrupted me on my way to her."

"Barker, there's nobody I'd rather have attending her than you. Get down there and save her."

Leif veiled his eyes. "I always do my best. No matter who the patient is."

"I know that. But for the sake of the Forerunner, do better than your best."

There was agony in his voice.

"Whatever can be done, will be," said Leif.

He went to flick the switch that would cut them off, something nobody but himself would have dared do.

Dannto said, "Wait! I understand she was in an automatic taxi. I suspect unreal conduct on the part of the techs at the control center. So I've put Candleman on the case. He'll probably be down very shortly. Give him every aid so that we may track down the culprits. I'll be down in a few hours. Just as soon as I can get the clearance. You've complete charge of Halla."

"Shib, *abba*," said Leif. "Does that include precedence over Candleman?"

"I said complete, Barker."

Chapter 4

LEIF TURNED OFF the QB and strode through the halls vaguely conscious that the nurses felt admiration towards him, that they liked his strength, broad shoulders, curly yellow hair, easy smile. He talked and laughed without fear and did not try to catch them in some unreality or other. When he was around, they could unstring their muscles for a while and feel bright and human.

He halted an elevator going up and stepped in. The nurse standing in it said, "Have you heard that Mrs. Dannto's been hurt?"

"That seems to be a very big secret," said Leif dryly. "I'm taking the car over because I'm on my way down there. You don't mind?"

She raised her eyebrows. "Would it make any difference?"

He pressed the button that sent it sliding downwards at emergency speed. "Not just now, Sarah. What else have you heard?"

"Dr. Trausti says she's dead."

Leif cursed inwardly, but he smiled.

"Mrs. Dannto can't die unless I give the official pronouncement, Sarah. And while I know it's unethical to question another doctor's judgement, it's possible that being human, he's made a mistake. Also, being too busy to do much reading, he may not have learned of a new technique that has been very successful in ferreting out the dying spark of life in patients who have already been pronounced dead."

He lied, of course. But Sarah's mouth was as big as it looked. In a short time after he'd gone into room 113, she'd have spread it all through the hospital that that wonderful Dr. Barker was using a miraculous technique to bring Mrs. Dannto back from the dead. By the time the story got to the ends of Rigorous Mercy Hospital, it would have Halla Dannto hurrying out the front door on her way to a tennis match.

Leif stepped from the car and sped down the hall. He found 113 closed and knocked on the door. A group of nurses and orderlies were standing near. He shot a look like buckshot. They scattered.

Trausti opened the door. His long black hair fell down across his high, narrow forehead. He brushed it aside muttering, "There's something very strange here, Doctor."

Leif stepped inside the room, noting as he did so the sheet-draped form on the cart beside the wall.

"Something strange?" he said to Trausti. He managed to put a slightly menacing tone in his voice as if he suspected that Trausti might be implicated in something not routine.

Trausti must have detected the tone, for the hands holding a strip of film trembled.

"Pardon me, Doctor Barker," he said. "I mean, something is definitely out of the ordinary. At least, I think it is. That is—well, I don't mean anything. I will allow you to make the decision."

Leif's eyebrows rose. "Allow?"

Trausti became even more flustered. "I—I mean that—well, I mean that I wanted to call to your attention something I do not understand."

"Ah, I see," said Leif, his tone indicating that he did not see at all. "Well, what is it?"

He was laughing inside himself, for Trausti mercilessly bullied the nurses and interns under him. Leif liked to keep Trausti off balance, keep him worrying. He suspected Trausti was spying on him for the Uzzites and he hoped someday to get Trausti into a position where he, Leif, could turn him over to the Uzzites and thus get rid of the danger he represented. Plus also making life easier for the poor devils who had to submit to Trausti's hectoring.

"It's the X-rays I took of Mrs. Dannto," said Trausti. "Apparently she died of a broken back, but . . ."

"I'll render the official verdict of her demise," said Leif. "All I want from you is an account of this thing you called strange."

Trausti swallowed and said, "Shib, shib, Doctor Barker. However, I am required to give you my findings. You may do what you like then, of course. It is my official opinion, based on these X-rays, that she suffered a broken back, a broken left arm, two broken ribs, compound fractures of the thigh, a broken pelvis, a ruptured liver, and a wound in the solar plexus. You may check my findings when you examine those films."

He pointed to a row of strips clipped to a large board.

"However, these films—" he waived the strip in his hands—"show something that I—forgive me if I am wrong—think is rather . . . uh . . . odd. This film is an X-ray I took of the uterogenital region."

Leif took the film from Trausti's shaking hand and held it up against the light from the wall. He saw at once what Trausti had meant. A tubular curving body occupied the posterior fornix, the recess behind the neck of the uterus where the upper portion of the vagina surrounded the vaginal portion of the uterus.

Leif put the film in his pocket and said, "Probably a growth. Whatever it is, it can wait examination until Mrs. Dannto is out of danger."

He did not know if the growth was a tumor or cancer or something else. But he wanted to squelch curiosity on Trausti's part.

Trausti handed him the second film with a shaking hand.

"This is an interior shot of the front part of the head."

Leif held the strip up to the light—and almost dropped it.

The film, though called an X-ray because of tradition, actually was the reproduction of images formed by the absorption of ultrasonic beams by organs. This film was one of a series which had photographed the interior of the head in one millimeter stages from front to back. The picture was plain enough. Two nerve cables ran from the posterior of the skull's frontal bone through the cranial dura mater or protective membrane of the brain. There the two cables were lost in the network of the brain's frontal lobe.

The nerve cables had no business being there! Leif had never seen anything like them.

Outwardly nonchalant, but inwardly shaken, Lief also put the second film in his jacket pocket.

"I've seen a case like this before," he lied. "Also a female. The dissection showed that nerve cables were mutations. However, since Mrs. Dannto is not dead, we won't be able to dissect her, will we?"

He paused, narrowed his eyes, and said harshly, "Do you have Mrs. Dannto's medical history?"

Trausti swallowed several times. "N—no. I did not think it was necessary to send for her records, since she is obviously dead. At least, I thought . . ."

"Have her history radioed at once from Montreal!" said Leif. "You have been guilty of unrealistic conduct, namely, assumption of too much authority and negligence. How can I treat her without an adequate knowledge of her medical background?"

Trausti looked as if he were going to strangle. After a struggle, he said, "Then you think . . . ?"

"I think we medical lamechians know more than you lower order of doctors," said Leif. "We have techniques available for the members of the hierarchy, which are denied to the lower classes because they do not deserve them. Tell me, has anyone besides yourself and Mrs. Palsson seen the X-rays?"

Trausti shook his head, his black hair falling across his eyes.

"I suggest," said Leif, "that you two keep this to yourselves. It might be that the Archurielite would not like it to get out that his wife is not quite normal. In fact, I *know* he wouldn't. He might reward loose talk with a trip to H."

Trausti, naturally as pale as a fish's belly, managed to whiten even more.

"I'll tell Mrs. Palsson."

"Do so at once," said Leif. "I'll take care of Mrs. Dannto from here on. You're through with the case."

Despairingly, Trausti said, "But she's dead!"

"Perhaps. Close the door as you go out."

Leif pulled the sheet back all the way to expose the naked and broken form of Halla Dannto. He sank his index finger in the wound on her solar plexus. It sank full length without resistance. That wound alone was enough to have killed her instantly.

Both Trausti and Palsson had seen her. What would they think? More important, what would they do, when they heard that Mrs. Dannto was convalescing from nothing more serious than a few broken bones, a slightly gashed solar plexus, and shock?

He cursed the Cold War Corps and its cell idea, where one man often hadn't the slightest hint of the overall plan and worked in the dark to carry out his particular segment. Here he was, a colonel of the March Republic CWC, originator of the plot that would probably send the Haijac Union to oblivion. And yet he wasn't allowed to catch more than a glimmering of the workings of his own campaign!

It was the price he must pay for working in the enemy's midst. If he'd allowed the brass to push him behind a desk down in Marsey, he could have seen the war as a whole; he'd been directing it. But since he insisted he wanted to work in Paris, where the danger was, he'd been sent there. Youthful folly! That was twelve years ago. He'd been twenty-two and had just been handed his surgeon's license and a second lieutenant's buttons. Now, big-bottomed fourstars with not half his brains were telling him what to do! Those modest thoughts raced through his head as he ran his hands over the once firm and vibrant flesh. Trausti was right. The X-ray had indicated something very strange, something that might or might not be connected with Project Moth and Rust. He suspected it was. Whether or not it was, he meant to find out what the foreign objects in her body were.

Two knocks sounded at the door. A pause. Three knocks.

Ava.

He opened the door. Ava entered the room. Ava was short and dark-haired and clad in a white uniform with a white collar and a skirt that fell to the ankles. Ava had long wavy hair which was braided and coiled on top of the head and eyes so large, liquid and soft they looked as if a speck of dust lighting on them would sink into their depths.

Ava said, in a husky voice, "What's going on, Leif?"

He told her what had happened.

Ava said, "What do you intend to do with her body?"

"I'd like to find out what the CWC is doing behind our backs," he said. "That is, if it *is* the CWC that's doing this."

"You misunderstand me," said Ava. "Should you be dissecting her now? You said the orders were to cremate her body as fast as possible, and no questions asked."

He shrugged and said, "As a surgeon, I'd give my coccyx to see what those growths really are."

"You'll lose more than your coccyx if the Jacks find out who you are. Or, for that matter, if General Itskowitz finds out you're not following orders."

He laughed big and booming.

"Little watchdog, I do believe you'd turn me in to him. My own wife."

"Cut it," Ava said. "We're wasting time."

"You're right." Leif covered the corpse again but the cloth fell around her curves to reveal a shape obviously feminine. He was forced to turn her on her side and throw another sheet from the bed over her, crumpling it somewhat to hide the form beneath it as much as he could.

"Our problem is to get her down to the PM without anybody knowing whose corpse it is," he said. "Anyone die on this floor recently?"

Ava nodded.

Leif said, "Don't use the QB. You'd better go to the desk and look through the book yourself. If you call to ask about recent deaths, somebody might get suspicious."

Ava nodded and left the room. Leif took out his pliers, which had a screwdriver on one end, and unscrewed the QB box. It took his practised hand only a moment to loosen the wire and make the box inoperative. He didn't want anybody to be able to look into the room and see what was going on.

Chapter 5

THE YEAR WAS 245 A.R. (After the Revelation) or, in the old chronology, 2700 A.D. It was exactly six hundred and forty years since three-fourths of mankind on Earth had been wiped out during the brief, undeclared war with the rebelling Martian colony. The Earthmen on Mars, who thought of themselves as Martians, had secretly introduced a laboratory-bred virus among Earthmen. This virus caused a virulent form of sickle-cell anemia, which in three months had killed six billion people. By good luck or because of unknown factors, the only comparatively large communities left on Earth were in Iceland, Israel, Australia, Hawaii, the Caucasian mountains of Russia, the Indonesian islands, and central Africa. Within a century the descendants of the surviving communities had exploded outwards, seizing all the relatively uninhabited territory and absorbing the local population.

Isaac Sigmen was born in 2455 A.D. in Montreal, Canada, of an Icelandic father and an American-Caucasian mother. In 1 A.R. he announced the revelation of a scientifically provable religion and his own ability to travel in time. Though mocked and persecuted at first, the Forerunner, as he titled himself, had established such a strong church in fifteen years that he eventually became head of the government of the Republic of America. The Republic included North and South America, the Pacific islands, and Japan, which had been colonized by English-speaking peoples from Hawaii and Australia. In another five years his religion had swept the Icelandic Republic, which included Iceland, England, Ireland, and all of northern Europe except the former country of Russia. Russia, Siberia, and northern China were colonized by Georgian-speaking peoples of the nation of the Caucasian Federation. In another two years, the Caucasian Federation was converted to Sigmen's religion. The Haijac Union (from Hawaii, Australia, Iceland, Japan, America, and Caucasia) was formed.

The other large nations of Earth were the Malay Democracy (Indonesia, India, southeastern Asia, southern China), Bantuland (Africa south of the Sahara Sea), and the Israeli Republic (the former Mediterranean nations and Asia Minor.)

There was one comparatively small country, which had been formed only fifty years before Leif Barker's birth. This was March, so-called because for centuries it had been a neutral zone between the Israeli Republics and the European frontier of Iceland. Neither country had dared seize it because of retaliation, so the strip had been declared neutral while both negotiated for possession of it. The result had been that for several centuries those liberals who affronted the governments of either of the negotiating parties, criminals, and men who had disliked the policies of their governments, had settled there. In time March came to assume the position Switzerland had once held, a neutral zone where nations could spy and intrigue against each other. Eventually, a government had been formed, and March declared itself an independent nation. March was composed of the former southern France, transalpine Italy, Switzerland, Austria, northern Yugoslavia, and southern Hungary. Its citizens, like those of old Switzerland, spoke four official tongues: English, Icelandic, Italic Hebrew, and Lingo, a strange and wonderful mélange of the first three.

Doctor Leif Barker was typical of a citizen of March. His father was American-Israeli and his mother was Icelandic-Caucasian. He had been born and raised in the city of Marsey (once Marseilles) and earned his M.D. at the University of Ven (once Vienna).

While at the university, he had conceived the plan for Project Moth and Rust. Fortunately, Leif Barker was able to get somebody high in the March government to listen to his plan and to put it into effect. His uncle was First Consul of the Department of Midi of the Free State of March, a position second only in power to the President. The plan had been initiated, and Leif, after proper training, was sent via the March underground to Paris. There, in the capital city of the West European Sector of the Haijac Union, in ancient Paris, he had worked his way up to Chief Surgeon of the Rigorous Mercy Hospital. And to colonel of the Cold War Corps of the Intelligence Branch of the Free State of March.

Chapter 6

BY THE TIME Leif had screwed the QB box back on, Ava had returned. "We're lucky," Ava said. "A man named Helgi Ingolf died ten minutes ago in 121."

"Does he go to PM?"

"Yes. He died raving and in a straitjacket, so Shant is going to do a head-post. He suspects a brain tumor."

"Good. Straitjacket? Ava, take that jacket off Ingolf. Bring it here. And while you're in Ingolf's room, call the floor above this and tell them our orderlies are busy and that you want two orderlies down here to wheel Ingolf's body to PM. Take Ingolf's tag from his toe—if there is a tag—and bring it here. I'll tag Halla's body with his.

"You're still carrying that stiletto in your well-padded bra, aren't you? Carve a J.C. on Ingolf's chest. We're going to do a job of confusion again."

"J.C. again?" Ava said.

"Shib. Hurry."

While Ava was gone, Leif examined Halla Dannto

more closely. What he found this second time convinced him that he could not allow her body to go into the furnace without a thorough dissection.

Ava returned with the straitjacket concealed under a blanket.

"You're using this so you can conceal the fact she's a woman?"

"You're so clever, honeypot," he murmured. "Though I doubt if we can really disguise her entirely. Would you be able to strap down the Himalayas?"

"Leif, sometimes you're revolting. Have you no respect for the dead?"

"No," he said. "If she were alive, she'd get every gram of respect that I've got. She's all woman. In fact, I don't think I've ever seen her equal, quick or not. Now, don't get jealous, dear."

Ava sneered, and then both bent to their work.

They strapped Halla down and covered her again with the sheet.

"Still a woman. Well, turn her on her side again. And cover that foot so only the tag sticks out," ordered Leif.

"Listen, did you get the names of the two orderlies from 200? If they seem too curious, we'll have to find a basis for unreal thinking on their part and turn them in to the Uzzites. Or arrange an "accident" through Zack.

"That reminds me. Trausti and Palsson saw the wound in her solar plexus. When her replacement gets here, they're going to wonder about that."

"Tsawah!"

"Ah, ah, Ava. No Hebrew. Especially no bad words."

"What I said goes for you, too," Ava said. "I'll say they're going to wonder! What'll we do? We can't accuse them of sabotage, for then they *will* talk. There've been too many *accidents*."

"What'll we do with the drunken sailor?" hummed Leif.

"Doesn't it worry you?" said Ava.

"Never worry about me worrying," replied Leif. "I'm just big and happy-go-lucky. I don't think they'll talk. I put the fear of God in them, that is to say, of his earthly representative in Paris, Mrs. Dannto's husband himself. They know something's up, but they're afraid of offending his nibs."

"Will it work?"

"If it doesn't," he replied, "then—" He drew his rigid index finger across his throat.

"Ava, here's what we do. Those two orderlies will wheel her body to the PM. I'll go along to make sure they note it's Ingolf's tag on the toe. I won't let them handle the body, because they'd be sure to know female. I'll tell them to leave the cart in the PM, that Shant wants it that way because he's got to move the body around for some unknown reasons of his own. They'll believe that. Everybody thinks the pathologist's a little unshib anyway. Then I'll shove the body in the locker."

"Who's unshib now?" Ava cried. "Your orders are to cremate her as fast as possible. And why are you going along instead of me? Won't the orderlies think that's peculiar?"

"I'm going because I want to make sure she's not cremated," said Leif. "I couldn't trust you not to burn her. I'm going to take Halla Dannto apart, and nobody's going to stop me.

"As for the orderlies, I'll tell them Ingolf died of a brain growth, and I'm going to do a fast post. They'll not question that. I *am* a cerebral surgeon, remember."

"Good God!" said Ava. "You're jeopardizing twelve years' work of the CWC just because of your damned curiosity."

"Possibly," he said, half-shutting his eyes. "But

I've always wormed our way out of jams in the past, haven't I? And you wouldn't turn your own husband in, would you?"

"Damn right I would. I hate your guts!"

"I love yours," said Leif, laughing and slapping Ava playfully at the same time.

Ava's dark face became filled with hate. "You louse! You try that once again and I'll slug you."

"Temper, temper, little one. How well it becomes you! And how seductive you look. Well, let's go. Candleman might come here before we get rid of the body."

Ava forgot to be angry.

"Candleman's coming?"

"Yes. If Halla's replacement doesn't get here soon, she may as well not show at all. And then how do we explain the cremation of Halla?"

"They must have done a magnificent plastic job on her if she can fool Dannto," said Ava. "Or maybe she's a twin."

"Possibly," said Leif. "What I'd like to know is how she could get here so fast. Do they have doubles on tap?"

"Who knows?" shrugged Ava. "You'd better get Halla out of here."

Leif opened the door and looked out. Nobody in the hall.

"Wheel her out," he said.

Just as Ava pushed the cart into the hall, two white-smocked men came around the corner. Leif beckoned to them.

"Take Ingolf's body to the PM," he said. "I'll be down in a second to do a head-post, so I don't want you to put him on the slab. Just leave him on the cart."

He didn't think he should explain why. They were only orderlies; it would be acting out of his behavior pattern if he were to do so.

When the two had shoved the cart into the service elevator, Leif said, "Ava, you get Halla's replacement into bed as soon as she gets here. And if she comes while I'm still in the PM, call me. And tell the 100 orderlies to move Ingolf's body to the PM. I'll take the tag off Halla's toe so the 100 men won't get any funny ideas if they see it."

"We're quite the conspirators," said Ava. "We're getting so involved we're bound to be tripped up."

"Act like you're afraid of nobody," said Leif. "That'll get you out of any trouble in this country where everybody's scared."

"Yes, but these people can tell if you're afraid or not. They can't smell fear on *you*, because *you've* got the guts of an angel—or a devil. And I, to be frank, am always sweating with fear."

"Ava, you talk too much. But that's a common failing of women."

Ava looked furious. Leif laughed and walked down the hall to the elevator.

Down in the basement, he met orderlies as they came from the PM. "Everything shib?" he asked.

"Shib, *abba*."

He said, "Wait a minute," and he pulled a pack of Fruitful Times from his pocket.

"I don't smoke, of course," he said, touching the lamech on his chest. "But I carry these for those who do."

They lit up, slightly ill-at-ease, yet pleased because he would take time out to talk with them. Leif discussed this and that with them, mainly the increasing rumors about the possibility of Timestop and the Forerunner's return. Casually, he mentioned Ingolf and his interest in doing a head-post on him. He didn't have to ask the orderlies their names, for he knew everybody in the huge hospital who had worked there longer than a week. By the time they'd left, he'd convinced them that he was a *real* man in all senses of the word. And he'd left no doubt in their minds that the body was Ingolf's. If they were to be questioned later by the Uzzites, they'd swear to it.

As soon as the orderlies were out of sight, Leif entered the PM. He locked the door, took the sheet off the body, untied the straitjacket and put the packet in the cremator. Then he wheeled the cart to the slab and there rolled the body over onto the slab. After putting on a smock, face-mask, and surgeon's gloves, he selected several scalpels and a pair of Mayo's scissors from a rack. With the ease of long practice he made the incision in the corpse from the notch at the base of the neck to the pubic symphysis. He peeled the skin and muscles from the breastbone and ribs, and, after clipping the ribs free, he swung the whole up like a drawbridge.

For a moment, before covering the face of the corpse with the ribs, he looked at her. Even in blue-grey death, the jaw hanging slackly, the face retained a certain beauty.

He sighed because of the glory that was to be no more, thought of how this flesh had once been warm and pink, how this mouth had laughed and swung and kissed. Then, cursing himself because he had momentarily lost his professional objectivity, he lowered the ribs.

Swiftly he cut through to his destination.

He was enraptured by what he saw. No doubt of it! The object detected by the X-ray was no tumorous or cancerous growth; it was a well-organized body which had grown naturally in its present position.

A well-organized body, he thought. For what purpose? And what did its presence indicate? That Halla was a mutated human being? Or that she was an extra-Terrestrial?

Ever since Trausti had shown him the X-rays, Leif had had a theory that Halla Dannto was of non-

Earth origin. It seemed to him a possibility that the Cold War Corps of March might have contacted hitherto unknown sapients on some just discovered interstellar planet, and were using them in the cold war against the Jacks. The CWC might be utilizing the sapients because they possessed powers, or advantages Terrestrials did not have. And the strange organs of Halla were connected with these powers and advantages.

There could be another explanation. But he could not think of any others.

No time for theories. Find out something about the function of the organ now, if possible. He couldn't proceed at his leisure, for he had to hurry back to make sure the dead woman's replacement appeared. Afterwards, he could return for a more thorough examination.

Leif quickly lowered a microscope from the ceiling. This was a bulky instrument with a small control panel and a hooded viewer. Through the viewer, which was at right angles to the object to be scrutinized, he could see the magnification of the organ. And he could see that nerves ran from the grey red-black spotted organ. They ran from the anterior end of the organ along the wall of the vaginal canal almost to the opening.

Leif moved the microscope back and forth while he studied the organ and nerves in detail. He was puzzled. But, obeying a sudden intuition—one of the "hunches" which, coupled with his skill, had made him a great doctor—he swung the microscope back towards the ceiling. From a shelf he took an instrument designed to detect the flow of bio-electricity, the current generated by living cells. It was possible that this organ was not dead yet. If he were to hold the two-pronged tip of the detector against the organ and then rhythmically squeeze the organ with the two fingers of his other hand . . .

"Ah!" he breathed. With every squeeze of his fingers on the organ, the meter on the detector indicated four hundred milliamperes.

His intuition had paid off! The organ was a biological source of electrical energy. It acted as a piezoelectric generator. When it contracted it released energy which traveled down the nerves along the vaginal canal.

He reasoned that the organ, in the living Halla, must have released the bio-electricity when it contracted under muscular action. And the muscular contractions, of course, were in turn affected by a nervous action. He did not know what the cause of triggering nerve action was, and he did not care to speculate. However, the four hundred milliamperes were an extremely strong bio-current, and the nerves that conducted it were very thick. What was the whole biological device for?

He could find out. The girl who'd be taking the place of the dead girl might be of the same kind!

The thought galvanized him. He hosed off the body, wrapped it in the sheet, and placed it in a drawer in the freezer. Then he locked the drawer and wheeled the empty cart out into the hall. There he found another cart with Ingolf's body beneath a sheet. He moved it into the PM, lifted the sheet to satisfy himself that Ava had cut two deep and large initials upon its chest and had left the stiletto struck in the side.

Evidently, Ava had given the orderlies instructions to leave the body outside in the hall. Supposedly, the men would think that Shant or some other doctor was busy inside and did not wish to be bothered.

Leif didn't like the setup. It was too complicated. Only the simple plans allowed you to see all the details in one sweep of the eyes. The complex plans were too hard to clean up. They left clues for the keen-nosed hounds of Uzzites to sniff out.

A good thing General Itskowitz couldn't see him now, he thought. He'd be yanked out of Paris and back to Marsey before you could say Jude Changer!

Chapter 7

WHEN HE STEPPED out of the elevator onto the floor 100, he saw that he'd delayed too long over Halla's body. A very tall man, half a head higher than Leif, was coming down the hall. He was stooped, and his thin neck was bent forward as if he were running to keep pace with the eager head. The face was long and narrow—hawk-nosed, thin-lipped, shadow-eyed. He looked like a blond Dante.

The Uzzite's slender hand with its transparent-skinned fingers was curled around the *crux ansata* handle of the whip stuck in his broad black belt. His eyes were grey beasts poised in the caverns beneath his tufted eyebrows. When they saw Leif, they did not lose any of their crouched-to-spring wariness.

"Candleman!" Leif cried.

The Uzzite dipped his beak in acknowledgment and walked on to the door of 113. When it would not open to his shove, he knocked on it.

Leif said, "You must make as little noise as possible. Mrs. Dannto is not to be disturbed."

Candleman's voice was deep. "She is still alive?"

Though his face did not change, he gave Leif the impression that he was surprised.

"Why not?" said Leif. "She's suffering from nothing more serious than a broken arm, a gash in the solar plexus, shock, and loss of considerable blood. Just now she's under a sedative."

"Strange," muttered Dante-face. "I was told she was dead or dying."

"Who told you that?" demanded Leif sharply. If Trausti or Palsson had been talking . . .

"One of my men. He came to the scene of the accident shortly after it happened. And he was certain that Mrs. Dannto couldn't live."

"Your men are not medically trained," said Leif. His eyes clashed with Candleman's.

"I want to see her and satisfy myself that she's all right," said the Uzzite.

"You may take my word for it," said Leif.

"I insist."

"I am her physician," said Leif. "I have Dannto's word for it that I'm to be in complete charge of her case."

"Dannto?"

"Yes."

Candleman took the seven-thonged whip from his belt and began to swish it with gentle menace through the air. He said, "Very well, then, but I can, at least, see her through the QB."

"It's not working," said Leif.

He grinned.

Candleman stared bleakly; it was probably the first time anybody had dared to mock him.

"Why?"

"Ask the tech responsible."

"Who is he?"

"I don't know," said Leif. "But I can tell you the names of all the techs in this hospital. It's easy because we've only six. And we need four times that number."

Candleman said, "I know there's a shortage of techs. Everything seems to be breaking down nowadays, and we haven't enough men for repair. We need new and larger schools for techs."

"Why should young men go into them when the tech professions are so hazardous?"

"What do you mean?"

"This," said Leif, heart pounding delightedly at this baiting. "If anything breaks down, the machinery is not suspected. No. The tech is. He is at once under the suspicion of sabotage. He is thought to be an enemy of reality, perhaps even a paid agent of the Izzies or the Marchers. He is hauled off and questioned. While he's being held, the additional burden of maintenance and repair falls on the shoulders of his already overburdened co-workers. If he can't answer the Uzzites satisfactorily—and their questions are so phrased that even if he's innocent he's likely to get rattled and not give the correct ones—he's sent to H. Whatever that is.

"If he is released, he's still under surveillance. That puts him under a nervous strain. If more breakdowns occur—and they're bound to, because of the present shortage of techs and materials—he'll get blamed. Back he goes to the Uzzite rooms, and so on. The result is that many of the techs are quitting, or trying to. The Sturch won't allow them to, of course, unless there's been a lowering in their efficiency or moral rating. The tech is, as the saying goes, caught between Forerunner and Backrunner. If he deliberately lowers his efficiency, he's accused of unreality. And so on. It's true he can conduct himself so that his gapt gives him a lower moral rating, and he'll be dismissed to the ranks of the unskilled.

"But that means a harder life, smaller living quar-

ters, less food, less prestige. He doesn't want to do
that so he stays on his job. But he's nervous. His
work suffers. He's investigated. Back he goes to the
Uzzite questioning rooms.''

Leif was talking as much as he could. He wanted to
keep Candleman busy.

Candleman swished the thongs through the air.

"Am I to understand you are criticizing the
Sturch?''

Leif rubbed his lamech. "When I'm wearing this?
You know that that's impossible! No, I'm merely
telling you why techs are hard to find.''

Candleman turned and called, "Thorleifsson!''

A stocky young man with a square hard face
stepped from around the corner. Leif recognized him
as one of the men whom he had anesthetized in the
waiting room of his penthouse last night. The three
Uzzites had recovered and fled before Leif was
through with the girl sent to trap him.

"Yes, *abba*,'' said Thorleifsson.

"Find out the tech responsible for the QB maintenance on this floor. Ask him a few questions about
the QB in room 113, but make no arrests. We might
want to detain him later, though.''

The lieutenant saluted and left. Candleman
wheeled on Leif and said, "Sandalphon asked me to
investigate this case. I can't intrude upon your
medical handling of his wife, but I can demand that
you at least allow me to satisy myself that Mrs.
Dannto is in that room.''

The doctor's brows rose.

"Just what do you mean by that?''

"Barker, I'm a man who *never* takes anything for
granted. I've only your word that she's in there. I
trust no man's word. Only my own eyes.''

"There are some things you've got to take on
trust—or go insane,'' said Leif.

He called softly through the door. "Ava. Let me in."

He hoped Ava would have sense enough to realize why he wasn't using their code knocks. He didn't want to take a chance on giving that away to the human bloodhound whose eyes he could feel biting his back.

The door swung part way open. He grabbed the knob with a firm grip so it wouldn't open any further and let himself in, edgewise. Candleman stepped up close and peered over Leif's shoulder.

"There she is," said Leif. "Are you satisfied?"

Candleman should have been satisfied. The woman in bed had the same mass of rich auburn hair that Halla Dannto had. And the face, in the dim light, looked exactly like the dead woman's.

Candleman said nothing but sucked in his breath. He was still staring when Leif shut the door in his face.

On the other side of the door, the doctor breathed relief. "When did she get here?"

"About a minute after you left. I thought you were never coming back."

Leif walked over to the bed. The woman had opened her eyes and given him a half-smile. He smiled back, but he felt that this was the cap to all the shocks he'd gotten that day.

This girl was a live ringer for Halla in more than one way. She tolled bells; except for the dead woman, he'd never seen such beauty.

"Have you any messages for me?" he asked.

"None except that you're to call me Halla all the time—until my sister recovers from her accident and takes back her proper place."

Leif hoped he hid his surprise. So they hadn't told her the truth. Poor girl. It was what had to be done, though. If she had to struggle to hide her grief while carrying out this deception . . . he shrugged and hoped he wouldn't have to be the one to tell her. He couldn't stand a woman's tears—if they flowed from a genuine emotion.

"Ava," he said, "I see you've put a splint on her arm. That was smart, but it might not be enough. We may have to carry this out to a realistic conclusion."

Ava spoke over the commie. Leif picked up the sheet over Halla and laid it aside. Her large grey-blue eyes widened, and she opened her mouth.

He said, "Untie that gown, will you? It's necessary that I examine you."

"Why should it be?"

Her voice even when alarmed, as now, was a creamy contralto. It had fingers that knew where his nerves were and plucked them like harp strings so that a delicious chill ran down his spine.

"Your sister was injured in certain places," he said. "Trausti saw her, and he knows where she was hurt. I've got to determine just how I can duplicate the appearance of those injuries without actually hurting you."

He hoped it sounded plausible. Whether it did or not, he was determined to check the resemblances between the impostor and her dead sister.

"But who besides you is going to check on those injuries?" she asked. "Mrs. Barker and yourself will be the only ones."

"You're not acquainted with medical procedures," he said. "We've not the time to argue. As your superior, I order you to disrobe. Believe me," he said, smiling to soften the effect, "I don't like to command you. But it's necessary."

Ava turned from the commie and watched him. Ava was probably wondering just what he was up to.

Halla showed no signs of obeying him. Leif said, in English, "Halla, I won't hurt you. I'm L. Barker and no bite."

She tried to stifle the giggle, but it came out anyway.

Still smiling, Leif reached out to untie the cords of the unlovely hospital robe. The spurious Halla brought up her leg and kneed him expertly in the chin. Half stunned, he reeled back.

Ava laughed and said, "You lecherous goat! That's good enough for you!"

Leif, holding his jaw, mumbled, "My first contact with you has impressed me very much. I hope you didn't hurt your knee?"

She laughed again, and the vocal fingers strummed something deep within him.

"I think I like you, Dr. Barker, even if you're up to no good and consider yourself something of a Don Juan. If I have to be examined like a fatted calf, let your wife do it. You see, doctor, I know *why* you want to scrutinize me."

"Then you know my reason is purely professional."

"No. Not purely," she answered.

Leif turned to Ava. "Lucky girl." Ava's black eyes sizzled.

He laughed as if at a secret joke, and when Ava scowled, he slapped Ava lightly in mock rebuke.

"For the sake of the Forerunner, be serious, Leif," said Ava.

"The only thing I'm serious about is not being serious," he replied. "Listen, dear, I'm going back to PM. I've some unfinished business there—" he gestured significantly at Halla—"and I'll be back as quickly as possible. Whatever happens, keep Candleman out."

"Why in H didn't you do it when you were down there?" Ava demanded.

Leif said, "I know I'm doing wrong, but I can't help myself. The scientist has triumphed over the soldier."

He turned to give his "patient" one last glance. She had sat up and thrown her back with a toss of her head. She looked as proud as a queen is supposed to look. Leif opened the door and slipped quietly out, knowing that never again would he be able to leave her without a sense of loss. He'd never felt that way before about any woman.

Before he went to the PM, Leif stopped off at the pathologist's office. There was a chance that Shant might be wanting to do a post on Ingolf at once. Leif intended to tell him that he was going to open the man's skull himself. Shant was one of the few persons in the hospital he didn't like; he made no pretense otherwise. It wouldn't be the first time he'd cut the pathologist out of an interesting post.

He hadn't used the QB to call Shant because he imagined that Candleman had put a censor on it. He didn't want anybody storming in on him while he was PM-ing the real Halla.

Shant was gone. Leif feigned a certain degree of displeasure because he wasn't there when wanted, and then he left. The secretary would tell Shant about it, and the pathologist would keep out of his way for a few days.

When he got to the PM door, he checked the spy-register. It showed nothing. That wasn't surprising, for someone had wiped the magnetic tape clean. A little dial in one corner of the box indicated that that had taken place less than three minutes ago.

Leif was glad he'd insisted on Ava's installing that device. Checking was good; doublechecking, even better.

The door was locked. Either the person who'd entered had wiped the tape after he'd left the room, or else had obtained a key from one of the authorities. The latter was more probable, which meant that the stranger was an Uzzite. Candleman, or one of his lieutenants, was on the prowl.

Leif didn't hesitate. He inserted the key and pressed the little button at its end. The other end emitted a frequency which neutralized the magnetic field that locked the metal edges of the door with the steel doorframe. Leif was taking a chance, for if the prowler within had taken the trouble, he could be warned of anyone entering. Uzzites wore wristboxes with such warning devices. Set to the door's frequency, they would emit an alarm should another key of the same frequency be turned on nearby.

Knowing the Uzzite's arrogance, Leif doubted if the officer would bother. After all, they had the right to enter any place except a lamech-bearer's home.

He was right. As he silently swung the door shut behind him, he saw Thorleifsson's chunky form bending over the end of the drawer that held the body of the original Halla. His key had unlocked the box; he was just beginning to slide it out.

Ingolf's unsheeted form was lying beneath the harsh central lights. The stiletto projected from his ribs, and the deeply gashed initials could be seen across the room. Thorleifsson had made quite a discovery.

Uzzites carried minimatics whose explosive bullets, though capable only of short range, would make a big hole in any man they struck. Leif didn't give him a chance to use it. As he strode catfooted toward the bent back, he drew a long scalpel from his inside coatpocket.

Leif had gained a certain reputation for eccentricity, a highly calculated one. For one thing, he refused to wear the calf-length boots of the average doctor. He preferred sneakers. His fellow workers thought it was comfort he had in mind. They were half-right. Silence was what he mainly wanted, and what he got now as he approached the broad back.

Leif could not have made a noise to attract Thorleifsson's attention. The Uzzite must have looked around because he was trained to be always suspicious.

Leif rushed Thorleifsson with his scalpel held before him. Thorleifsson grunted, and his hand flashed down towards the minimatic in the holster on his belt. Then, seeing that Barker was too close for him to draw his gun in time, Thorleifsson threw up one hand to knock the scalpel away. He was partly successful. He did keep the weapon from entering his throat. But he had to pay for his partial success. The scalpel entered his palm and drove through the back of his hand.

Thorleifsson grunted again, and he reached with his other hand for the handle of the scalpel. Evidently, he meant to pull it loose.

Leif, however, had not stopped his charge. He slammed into the Uzzite and went down with him to the floor. Again, Thorleifsson grunted. Some of his wind had been knocked out. But he was too heavy and strong to be checked even by the wound and the impact. With his uninjured hand he tried to seize Leif's genitals and crush them.

Leif blocked the move by writhing away, but he lost his position on top.

Thorleifsson rolled away, jumped up, and reached again for his minimatic.

Leif launched himself through the air, feet first. He kicked out, and the toe of his sneaker struck the hand that had just drawn the gun. The gun flew away.

Thorleifsson was, for a second, motionless, his left hand useless because the scalpel pierced it; his right, because of the kick against his wrist. Then Thorleifsson, silent as he had been since Leif entered the room, raised his hand to his mouth and bit down on the handle of the scalpel. And with a backward jerk of his head and a forward jerk of his hand, he pulled the scalpel loose. His expression did not change.

Leif, after the kick, had managed to land on one foot and thus kept himself from falling on his back. For a second, he paused, and that was enough time for Thorleifsson to regain control of his right hand. Thorleifsson took the scalpel from his mouth and advanced, crouching, on Leif.

Leif was undecided whether to run for the minimatic, which had fallen in the near corner of the room or continue his direct attack.

The Uzzite decided for Leif. He stepped between Leif and the gun, and for the first time he spoke.

"You . . . you filthy monster! How can you wear that—" he pointed with his bleeding hand at the golden lamech on Leif's chest—"and yet be a traitor?"

"What makes you think *I'm* the traitor?" said Leif. "Don't you know that you have been denounced as an unrealist and that your fellow Uzzites are looking for you?"

Thorleifsson's face turned grey. The scalpel lowered.

"What? How could it be?"

Leif acted before Thorleifsson could recover from the shock of the lie. He tore the lamech from his shirtfront and threw it at the Uzzite's face. The heavy golden badget struck the man in the eye.

Thorleifsson did not cry out, perhaps because he was too stunned. Stunned because the accusation—which must have been unthinkable to him—paralyzed him, or because a lamech had been thrown at him. The lamech was a symbol invested with centuries of authority and holiness. Even a man as cynical as an Uzzite was inclined to be would not be able to overcome entirely the conditioned reflexes instilled in him as a child.

Whatever the reason, he moved too slowly to defend himself when Leif seized the hand that held the scalpel.

Leif twisted. Bones snapped. Thorleifsson cried out. The scalpel fell, but Leif caught it by the handle. He drove the point into Thorleifsson's bulging belly, turned the scalpel a half twist and pulled it out. And then he cut Thorleifsson's throat.

Chapter 8

WHILE THORLEIFSSON'S FLESH and bones burned in the crematory, Leif removed all traces of blood from the floor and looked for anything else that might give away the Uzzite's presence. Then, he took Mrs. Dannto's body from the locker and placed it on the slab. As he worked he wondered about the lieutenant's appearance. Had Candleman sent him because he'd heard a report from Trausti? Or had one of the orderlies thought that Ingolf's body looked suspiciously curved beneath the sheet?

He didn't know. It might be anything. Whatever it was, Leif intended working until the last possible moment.

After he'd put on gown and mask and gloves, he prepared slides of blood and tissue. While the Lab-tech machine analyzed samples, Leif began his head-post, cutting fast. His time was short; he wouldn't be able to do a half-decent job. But he had to find out *something* about this strange woman.

Leif tried to shake off all interfering thoughts and concentrated on his work. Neither a philosopher nor morbidly inclined, he found himself oppressed by the silence, the harsh light, the cold, and the unresponsiveness of this pathetic specimen. Even the passion of the quest for knowledge did not absorb him enough. Soundless voices spoke; chill tongues chocked moribund syllables; the penetration of the steel evoked a fluttering of protest, a shapeless naysaying.

He was reminded of the encounter early that morning with the pale-eyed and flare-nostriled four and the impact of the *"Quo vadis?"* that had stopped him in mid stride. Any other time he'd have bayed after those unique creatures with the relentlessness of the indefatigably curious. He was sure they held the key to something, but the maddening squirrel cage he was trapped in wouldn't allow him to reach for it.

He must be getting weary. Those last two thoughts were as mixed in metaphor as you could get. On the other hand, what was life but one mixed metaphor after another?

He bent to his work. The mass of rich auburn hair rolled back under his fingers and thumbs. Underneath the soft flames was a thick and fat layer much like an orange peeling. He'd barely folded back the scalp before he was stopped by two small bumps hidden under her hair. They seemed to be composed of fatty tissue, perhaps nerve tissue. Leif severed them and inserted them in the Labtech for analysis; using the microscope, he viewed the holes left in her skull. The holes appeared to be the ends of nerve cables.

Excited, forgetting the apprehension of the moment before, he finished stripping her cranium and applied the roaring edge of a circular saw to her skull. His unorthodox cutting pattern was intended to expose as much of the brain as possible for a hasty examination. When the membrane of the dura mater was exposed, the brain was similar in structure to a

Terran's. But he was convinced that a closer examination would show many differences.

Fervently, he wished he had the chance to do some analysis. He didn't. There was nothing else to do but go on and note the more radical departures. However, he wasn't so fast that he escaped seeing that the nerves from the two scalp bumps connected both to the forebrain and the middle.

The Labtech clicked for attention. Leif ignored it. He would read its findings later, and all at once. He was determined now to know this woman as he'd never been determined to know a live woman.

She had been lovely as few women are, and now he, ruthless male, with the untiring and passionate knife, had deprived her of that loveliness in an even more shameful way than Death.

"Forerunner," he muttered to himself in the room's cold silence, "what's the matter with me? I'm no damn sentimental anthropomorphist, but something tonight has sure gotten into me."

He wondered if it could have been the reaction from killing the Uzzite. He doubted it, for he'd felt no revulsion at sinking the blade into that fat throat. The deed had been that of one soldier slaying another; both were acting in the line of duty. Besides, he'd deliberately murdered two high officials on the operating table. It had been his decision; he'd not done them on orders from Marsey. The two men had to be put out of the way so that CWC agents could move up in the hierarchy to take their place. Inasmuch as the two officials were lamech-bearers, they could not be accused of unreal thinking and thus sent to H. So Leif had murdered them. It was an indication of his professional ethics that he used the verb *murdered* and not a military euphemism.

Whatever was bothering him, it had sliced into his skin as surely as his knife was dividing flesh from flesh.

He shrugged again and bent over his work. The ribs had been raised, like a drawbridge. He counted twelve pair, true and false, the human number.

The heart, the lungs, the liver, and the kidneys were, as near as he could determine, thoroughly human. So were the muscular and skeletal systems. He removed an eyeball and deposited it in the Labtech for analysis. Five minutes later, the Labtech clicked a dozen times, and a yellow light on the front panel flashed. Leif read the tape that stuck like a perforated tongue from an orifice in the front panel. The report was the same as for the samples of blood and tissue. No abnormalities detectable. Which meant that the dead woman was a Terrestrial human being.

Leif had two contradictions to consider. One, the woman had two biological deviations from the norm of *homo sapiens*—the two growths on top of her head and the organ at the end of her vaginal canal. Two, it was almost beyond the limits of probability that an extraterrestrial female would so closely resemble an Earth female. Even the three types of humanoids found on other planets varied enough in external and internal characteristics for an untrained man to distinguish them in a glance. No XT would ever be mistaken, except at a distance, for a Terrestrial.

Yet, there was the unmistakable evidence of the alien organs.

And he did not think that mutation would account for them. They were too complex and well organized to be the result of genetic malfunction or deviation. No, the organs were alien.

And that reminded him that he had subjected to analysis by the Labtech machine a sample of every organ of Halla Dannto except that which had first aroused his curiosity. He had not wanted to put the organ into the machine, for that meant its destruction while it was being analyzed. Also, there were certain tests he wanted to give it which the machine could not.

However, he could not keep it for a personal scrutiny. He would have little chance to work on it in the laboratory without fear of being spied upon. And he could be very embarrassed if he were asked to explain what the organ was and where it came from. Even if he pulled rank an declined to answer, he would cause suspicion and possibly an investigation.

Sighing, he deposited the cylindrical mass of flesh and the attached nerve ganglia in the Labtech. He punched the controls which set the machine for the desired tests and then paced restlessly back and forth. Ten minutes later, the clicking sounded, the yellow light flashed, and a strip of tape thrust out from the recorder-hole.

Leif read the brief, coded message.

DATA LACKING. DIFFERENT QUESTIONS NEEDED.

"Too bad," muttered Leif. "I don't know what questions to ask."

Death and the knife had analyzed Halla. The questions he would like to ask were not for machines to answer. Life . . . death . . . and the narrow margin between. Why . . . why . . . how?

Pausing only for a silent reflection on the transience of beauty, Leif paid his respects to the dead woman, and consigned her remains to the crematorium.

The body burned, the Labtech's tapes wiped, Leif stripped off his working clothes and put them in the furnace. Then he hosed down the walls and the floors. The only object he did not cleanse was Ingolf, still waiting upon the cart. When the sterilization was complete, he pushed the corpse back into the hall and from there took the elevator up to 100.

There he found Candleman, standing motionless outside 113.

"Where have you been?"

Leif raised his brows.

"I consider that question impertinent," he said., "but since I am anxious to contribute to clearing up the mystery of this accident, I'll answer you."

Leif stepped to the door and knocked softly.

Candleman said harshly, "Well, aren't you going to speak?"

Leif pretended to start. "Ah, yes, I was preoccupied."

He watched the man for a sign of annoyance, but the face was as fixed as a gargoyle's.

"I've been dissecting a man who died of a brain tumor," he said. "Part of my work recently has been correlating changes in brain waves with injuries of certain parts of the brain. Most interesting."

Ava opened the door. At that moment a nurse, coming down the hall, called Leif. She held a slip of paper in her hand, and her brow was wrinkled.

Turning, his hand on the knob so Candleman couldn't get in, he said, "Yes?"

"Dr. Barker, the head nurse of 100 noticed a discrepancy here. Two orderlies from 200 were called down to remove a Mr. Ingolf's body to PM. But she knows that two of our men did that. She noticed the discrepancy when 200's supervisor QB'd her to ask if she'd check the orderlies' movements. She suspects one of unreality."

Leif let his breath out softly. He'd lost this round. There was a ninety-to-one chance that the discrepancy would never have been detected in the mass of quadruplicate reports. But one of the boys was thought to be unreal; a term that could cover anything from murder to laziness or stupidity. Probably the latter.

Candleman watched him closely, but that might not mean anything. Those fierce grey eyes fastened their claws on everything. There was a chance, however, that the Uzzite had told the nurse to carry this news to him so that he might surprise Leif in some telltale word or gesture.

He looked her in the face. Her bright profile was presented to the Uzzite; she must have felt safe, for her left eyelid winked. Candleman *had* put her up to it.

Leif's policy of making friends with the personnel had paid off. That she was willing to take a chance with the dreaded Uzzite's eyes on her warmed him. It just was not true, as some of his associates swore, that none of these people were worth saving.

"Well," said Candleman.

Leif shrugged. "What do you expect me to do about it?"

They glared into each other's eyes.

Impasse.

But at that moment the click of angry heels echoed down the hall. A little blond-headed man with a big nose bounced before Leif.

"Dr. Barker, what's this I hear about you doing a post on Ingolf?"

"That's true, Dr. Shant."

Shant shrilled, "You're crowding me, Dr. Barker! I asked that I be allowed to do the post."

"He died of cerebral tumor; I'd been eegieing him for several weeks," said Leif. "I was interested. Furthermore, as head gapt of this hospital, I don't have to get your permission."

Shant bounced up and down, tapdanced, heels clicking. "Nevertheless, you should have been ethical enough to ask me to assist."

"Shant, you weary me. Shuffle off, will you?"

Leif felt someone pushing the door from within. He stepped aside enough to let Ava by.

Ava's finger was on the lips; the big shimmering eyes were concerned.

"Gentlemen, I must ask you to be quiet. Mrs.

Dannto needs all the sleep she can get.''

Candleman flowed out of his crouch. Straightening his long back, he said, "You're right. The welfare of the Archurielite's wife comes first. I suggest, Dr. Barker, that you spend more time attending her and less to dissections.''

"I don't tell you how to conduct your profession. Please keep your long nose out of mine,'' snapped Leif.

Shant and the nurse gasped. You didn't talk to an Uzzite like that.

Candleman's face was passive as a wax dummy's.

"Anything that concerns the Archurielite is my business. And I'm beginning to think that some of your actions are very much my concern.''

"Think as you please.'' said Leif. He propelled Ava into the room and then stepped in after her.

When the door was shut, Ava said, "You fool!''

"Do you want me to cringe?'' said Leif. "How do you think I got where I am today? I tell you, if you act like you're not afraid, these people think you must be somebody, and they're scared of you.''

"You go too far.''

"Never mind. Remember, I'm your superior. Refrain from telling me off, even if you are—'' he laughed—"my wife.''

"Halla,'' he said to the girl as she sat up, "I want you to take a lotus pill.''

"Why should I?''

"Are you or are you not under my orders?''

"I am, as long as they don't interfere with my prime directives. One of them is to keep my real identity secret. I think you're showing too much curiosity.''

"Take this.''

"It's not a truth drug?''

"Take it. Or I'll break your arm while you're still conscious.''

Her eyes widened.

"You mean it?"

"Shib, I do. Do you think that bloodhound outside isn't going to check the X-ray files and see if your arm really is broken?"

"Why can't you pick out somebody's X-rays from the files and show them to him?"

"We can't take that chance. He'll check on that angle. We're in too much of a jam now. What with two Ingolfs and the fact that Trausti or Palsson might talk."

"Two Ingolfs?"

"Never mind," he said, as he realized he'd almost exposed the fact that her sister was dead. "The less you know about that, the better. You're supposed to be Mrs. Dannto, remember? Even if Ava and I are tripped up over something else, you keep on acting as if you only know us professionally."

"Do I look that stupid?"

Ava moved around Leif and began undoing the splint.

Halla paid Ava no attention, but looked straight at him.

"Will the break spoil the symmetry of my arm?"

He was surprised, not because a woman would wonder about disfigurement instead of pain, but because she should voice her concern without false modesty, so matter-of-factly.

"They'll never be able to tell the difference. In fact," he added, smiling, "it'll probably be straighter than before. Art improves on life, you know."

"No, I don't."

Chapter 9

A MOMENT AFTER Halla swallowed the pills and the water, her lids dropped, and she began breathing softly. Except for the flush in her cheeks and that indefinable look of fullness which the quick have and the dead lack, she was an exact facsimile of her twin as she had first lain on the slab.

He shoved a chair to her bedside, picked up her arm, laid it across the arm of the chair, grabbed her wrist and elbow, and brought the lower part of her limb against the hard plastic.

The sharp snap of the bone made him wince.

Without pausing, he reset the broken radius and ulna. Ava quickly splinted the forearm.

While Ava was doing that, Leif shot Jesper's serum into Halla's upper arm. If the hormone activator worked as fast as it usually did, the bone would be knit within two or three days.

"You've got the blueprints?" he asked.

Ava said, "No. They're over there."

"Get it ready, will you?"

He took out his scalpel, dipped it in a bottle of

sterilizer, and poured the liquid over a piece of cotton. Then he threw back the sheet and untied her gown so that her whole front was exposed. He swabbed her solar plexus with the dripping cotton, laid it down, and expertly gashed the skin to simulate the wounds.

Ava smeared a handful of jelly on the raw cuts; if no infection occurred, the torn tissue, stimulated by the jelly, would replace itself with a few days. There would be no scars.

"Give me that camera," he said. Ava handed it to him. He set the dials and shot two external photos and two internal, a pair for the arm and a pair for the gashes.

A minute later he took the developments from the box and looked at them.

"Fine. This ought to satisfy Candleman. But Trausti's pictures will be in the file, or in his pocket."

Ava smiled with beautiful white teeth.

"Oh, no. Not in his pockets," Ava said. "I picked them and desposited them in the sanctity of my bosom. See."

Ava's delicate fingers darted to the gap in the high-necked dress and pulled out two sheets of film.

"You darling," said Leif. "When did you do that?"

"I met him when I was on the way down here. He stopped me for a second to say that he was certain Mrs. Dannto was dead. His pictures proved it. He seemed quite proud to have caught you in a mistake."

Ava laughed and said, "Now, he won't be so full of baseless vanity."

"Better destroy it."

"Naturally. Leif, sometimes you act as if you were the only one with brains."

"Temper, temper, baby. Come here and I'll reward you with a big, juicy kiss."

"You'd not look so good with all your teeth knocked out."

He laughed. Bending over Halla, he resumed the examination she had once interrupted with a knee in his jaw.

"What's your interest in this babe?" asked Ava sourly.

"Jealous, honey?"

"Aargh," croaked Ava, asking no more, because it was hopeless.

Leif's fingers had felt the two small bumps hidden in the hair on top of her head. And the X-ray had shown him the organ which occupied the posterior fornix. He tied up her gown and replaced the sheet.

"She'll sleep for twelve hours. You stand guard. I have to go down to the PM again to clear up the Ingolf mess. Or make it worse. I'll relieve you later."

Abruptly, he wheeled.

"Oh, oh, fingerprints! I know I'm being overly cautious, but I wouldn't put it past Candleman to compare this Halla's prints with the other's."

"I'm ahead of you, Leif. You won't believe it. They're identical. She told me that while you were gone."

"The CWC has done a good job on her."

"My impression was that the two were born that way."

"Impossible."

"But true."

"What about retina-patterns?"

"The same, also."

Leif ran his hand through his thick yellow waves.

"Nothing that has happened since Rachel called me this morning has been believable. Well, ours not to question why, and you know the rest of that dismal line. I'm going, Ava."

"J.C.," said Ava, pointing her finger at him.

"J.C.," he replied, smiling and making a similar gesture.

When he walked into PM, he wasn't surprised to see Candleman and Shant. They were examining the recent records in the Labtech. Nearby, two sergeants were sprinkling powder over the walls and floors. Another was taking photos. A fourth had opened the cremator door and was vainly trying to scrape ashes from the thoroughly washed interior.

Seeing the doctor, the chief Uzzite straightened up and glared. He said in his monotone, "Why did you cremate Ingolf yourself, instead of leaving him for the assistants to burn?"

Leif smiled, safe in the assurance that he had several times previously done just that to other bodies and for the reason that he wanted it established as part of his behavior pattern in case such an emergency as the present arose.

"Candleman," he said, "I don't hold that a man in a post of authority loses face if he uses his hands for manual labor. We're short of help here in every way, and I like to save time. Check my efficiency ratings and my psych records, if you wish."

"I've a man doing that now," growled the chief.

"I thought we lamechians were above suspicion?"

"This is routine," said the chief.

Leif smiled.

He looked around and then decided he might as well drop his bomb now as later.

He called in an imperious tone to Shant.

"Doctor, whose body is that out in the hall?"

Shant's face crimsoned, and he said, "I—I—don't know. It was there when we came in."

"Well, wheel it in. You know it's against our policy to leave it out where its sight may depress people and give them unreal thoughts."

Shant clenched his fists, ground his teeth, and glanced at the Uzzites to see if they were watching his humiliation. But he walked stiff-legged into the hall and brought the cart and its burden into the PM. Idly, as if he weren't really interested, Shant picked up the tag to examine it.

His jaw dropped; so did the tag.

Candleman said, "What's the matter?" His storklike legs carried him towards the runty pathologist.

Shant threw off the sheet and exposed the face of the corpse so Candleman could see it.

"Jacques Cuze!" said Candleman. He halted in mid-stride as if someone had struck him in the face.

For the first time since he'd known him, Leif saw the man's face crumble. It was like a glacier falling into the sea.

"Thorleifsson!" bellowed Candleman. "Where is he?"

One of the sergeants stepped up to his agitated chief and whispered in his ear.

Candleman listened and then said, "Very well. But put out a QB for him. He shouldn't be prowling around unless I authorized it. He'll pay for this dereliction of duty."

Candleman, thought Leif, must really be upset. Leif didn't given him a chance to regain his balance. He, too, strode to the body. And looking at it, gasped, "That's Ingolf! The man I dissected!"

Shant blinked. "That's impossible! Obviously."

"So it is. But there he is. And less than an hour ago I saw him reduced to ashes.

Leif thought fast. He'd have to contact Zack Roe and tell him to order their agent in the Census Bureau to do some fast work. Candleman would undoubtedly take the finger-and-retina prints of the man on the cart and compare them with those in the files. The CWC agent could, before then, plant Ingolf's prints in the records of a man who'd been dead, say, a hundred years. Or better yet, a man who was the contemporary of the Forerunner. Two and a half centuries ago.

The filer would then "accidentally" discover this. The announcement would create a consternation, add to the mystery and the tensely superstitious air everybody was breathing now that the Forerunner was expected to stop time and return from his temporal travels.

Signs and wonders they wanted; let them have them.

The dunnologists would, of course, theorize that the dead man had two bodies in present time and one in the past because, he, too, was traveling in time. For years it'd been a near-dogma that if a man journeyed in time and then returned to a period where he'd once lived, he would find himself with a duplicate. Or with as many bodies as the times he returned.

Obviously, Ingolf had proved this beyond question.

But the case would be a hopeless paradox, one to be argued in the professional *Journal of Chronos* and *Fields of Presentation* and exploited by propagandists as adventure stories in the comics.

There would be in the mystery. Who, really, was Ingolf? What did the gashed initials mean? Why the stiletto? For Shant would soon find that the mutilations had been committed after Ingolf's death.

If Ingolf had died once two hundred and fifty years ago and twice today, and seemingly as a result of the activities of the notorious and nefarious J.C., who, then, was he? A disciple of the Forerunner? Had the wicked Backrunner, Sigmen's half-brother and immortal enemy, Jude Changer, killed him? Not once, but thrice? And would he do it again?

Or was it the feared underground Frenchman, Jacques Cuze, that shadowy and insane figure who clung to the idea that he could rid his beloved and long-lost country of the Forerunner's disciples?

"Jacques Cuze," said Candleman, echoing Leif's thought with his Icelandic pronunciation. "That man has been here under my nose. And I've allowed him to escape."

The grey shields of his eyes glared as is he thought the man were in the PM and waiting to stab him.

"Dr. Barker!" announced the QB. Leif strode to the wall and flicked the toggle.

"In the PM," he said.

"The Archurielite, Dr. Barker."

The girl's voice trembled.

"Don't get scared, sweetheart. He won't bite you."

Dannto's double chin appeared in the box, followed by the rest of him. Scowling, he said, "I heard that remark!"

"It's true, isn't it?"

"You know what I mean!" bellowed Dannto. Face red, he struggled with himself and then said, "Never mind that. How's my wife?"

"The first reports of the accident were very much exaggerated. She's not badly hurt at all. She'll be up and out of bed tomorrow. But just now you can't see her. I gave her a sedative that'll put her under for twelve hours."

"Can't I look at her on QB?"

"It's not working. And we don't want anybody in the room to disturb her."

"Not working? By Sigmen, somebody'll pay for this!" He looked over Leif's shoulder. "Candleman, have you investigated the tech responsible?"

"Shib, *abba*. But I can't find Lieutenant Thorleifsson. He was sent to question the fellow."

"Why can't you find him?"

"*Abba*, there is something very peculiar here."

Candleman, grey eyes steady, explained in his deep monotone.

When the Uzzite stepped back so Dannto could see the initials on Ingolf's chest, the Archurielite breathed, "Jude Changer!"

Dannto made a quick recovery.

"Where's the cordon you should have thrown up around the hospital?"

"I just now learned of Jacques Cuze's presence here," retorted Candleman. "And you've been monopolizing the QB since then."

"Jacques Cuze?" said Dannto. "This is clearly the work of Jude Changer."

"In that case," said Candleman, face rigid but voice tinged with anger, "a cordon would be useless. You can't pursue a man who slips in and out of time like a snake through the grass."

"It's your business to find out whether it is Jude or not," roared Dannto. "How do you know I'm right? You're an Uzzite; you take nobody's word."

Candleman blinked at the change of tactics, stepped up to the wall and cut off the priest's image. He dialed UHQ. "Captain, send forty men down to the Rigorous Mercy Hospital at once."

The captain tried to hide the comic he'd been reading and at the same time look calm and dignified.

"*Abba*, we haven't got that many men available."

"Get them down here in ten minutes."

"Shib, *abba*."

Ten minutes later, the Sandalphon, Dannto, entered the PM.

He waddled up to the Uzzite and put his treetrunk-thick arm around the bony shoulders.

"Jake, old man," he said. "I'm sorry I got angry with you. I know you're doing your best and that you're the most efficient of all Uzzites. But you must understand that I am very much concerned with Halla's welfare, and anything that affects her disturbs me very much. Moreover, the J.C. business is most upsetting. Those initials have been appearing with alarming frequency in the most unexpected and implausible places for the last three years. And, so far, we haven't found the person responsible for them."

Candleman stepped away so Dannto had to drop his arm. "I accept your apology," he said, "but you've got to understand that it's a very sore point with me. That man, Jacques Cuze, has been plaguing me so long and so persistently that I am about to let my other duties go and turn the attention of the whole department to the matter. I have something planned that will, I swear by Sigmen, catch him."

"I'm sure you will. *If* Jacques Cuze actually exists. Personally, I think he's a myth," replied Dannto. "I think Jude Changer is to blame for those initials."

"Perhaps you're both barking up the wrong tree," said Leif, smiling at his own temerity and inability to resist a pun. "Gentlemen, if we get off into a theological discussion, we'll be lost. Therre are more immediate things that deserve our attention.

"For one thing, *abba*, I'd like to get your permission to move your wife to the penthouse. Inasmuch as my wife is taking care of yours, it will be more convenient for both of them. And, moreover, as Candleman has hinted that the accident might not be one after all, I think she'll be a lot safer in our place."

Dannto whirled. "Not an accident? Candleman, you didn't tell me that!"

"Forgive me, *abba*. I didn't want to upset you."

"Who do you think is behind it?"

Candleman held out his big bony hands, palms up. "Jacques Cuze. Who else?"

"But why should he try to kill Halla?"

"Because through her he can hurt you. Because he is a devil, an unreal person."

"It would be like Jude Changer to do something like that," said Dannto. "According to what I've heard, he will stop at nothing in order to change real time into pseudo-time. Candleman, we've got to stop him."

"You have to give me carte blanche."

"You've got it."

"What about my request?" said Leif.

"Oh, certainly. Excellent idea. She'll be much safer and get better care there."

"And I'll have two men stationed at the entrance to your penthouse," said Candleman. "I don't want any repetition of the accident."

Leif replied, stiffly, "I think she'll be safe. I'll be there at all times."

"Nevertheless, I insist."

Leif shrugged and said to Dannto, "Would you like to come along while we move your wife? Later, we can eat at my place. I'm rather hungry, and we can discuss further details."

Dannto's cavernous belly rumbled. He laughed, though somewhat embarrassedly, and said, "There's your answer."

Chapter 10

WHILE HALLA WAS being moved, Leif noted that Dannto accepted the woman as his wife. He'd thought he would, but he still breathed relief. Later, after Halla had been put in one of the bedrooms, and a nurse installed with her, Leif, Ava, Dannto and Candleman sat down to eat. The latter had been invited by the Archurielite.

Candleman's eyes were grey nets, scooping up every detail of the penthouse. As he bent over his locust soup with loud sucking noises, he cocked his head this way and that to hear better what each said.

Leif guessed that both the maid who served them their food and the nurse now attending Halla had been briefed by the Uzzite. They could watch the doctor and his wife and report their every move. All as a matter of routine, of course. You didn't suspect a lamech-bearer of unreality.

"Leif," said Dannto, in a good mood now that he was filling his belly, "you remember that last month you diagnosed a beneficent tumor that had to come out. Why not do it now? I could spend the night here."

"Very good idea," said Leif. "You'll be fit for work by morning, if you want to."

He thought, what kind of hold did the original Halla have over this Robin Redbreast? She must have had something. She was the most beautiful woman he'd ever seen, but he knew that it took more than that to make a man devoted.

He wondered if her sister had the same.

He intended to find out.

Candleman sucked in the last of his soup and reached out for the grassbread.

"I must insist on being allowed to watch the operation," he said.

Leif replied coldly, "I think you're making too many hints concerning my unreality."

"I'm sure Candleman didn't mean that," said Dannto.

"Of course not," Candleman said in his deep monotone. "But how do I know that Jacques Cuze won't try something?"

"You'll have to watch the operation on the QB," said Leif. "It might make my assistants nervous to know the great Candleman's suspicious eye was on them. And nervous doctors and nurses are liable to make a fatal slip."

Candleman opened his mouth to protest, but Dannto stalled him.

"That's right, You'll do that, Jake."

The Uzzite's lips clamped.

"Shib. But I'll have men stationed outside the doors."

Leif made a mental note to have the QB go out of order during the operation. And wondered what good tech he'd frame for this job.

Peter Sorn was the victim. He'd been blamed for the breakdown of the QB in Halla's room. Let it happen again, the same day, and young Sorn would as likely as not, go to H.

Too bad. Leif like Peter Sorn. But he couldn't allow personal feelings to interfere. This was war, even if cold. Removing Sorn from the ranks of the techs would be one more step toward the realization of the March goal.

"How long will it take?" said Dannto.

"About half an hour. Maybe less. Afterward, you should get a good night's rest. In the morning the blue-print jelly will have healed you enough so you may resume your ordinary duties. No exertion, of course. Perhaps you'd better not stay in the same room with your wife tonight."

Dannto guffawed and slapped the table so the dishes and ware rattled.

Candleman dropped his spoon and glared at Leif. A flush crawled up from the high neck of his uniform.

"Your thoughts do not seem to be as pure as a lamechian's should be," he said.

Dannto chuckled. He turned to Leif. "Jake's a little oldfashioned."

"If being oldfashioned means rigidly and un-deviatingly following the teachings of Sigmen, real be his name, then I plead guilty," said Candleman.

"Well, such remarks as Leif just made aren't specifically forbidden," replied Dannto, his smile disappearing into the fat on his face. "However, you may be right."

Candleman raised his eyebrows slightly and said, "I feel that I've failed because, so far, I've gotten no clue as to who Jacques Cuze is or the extent of his organization. But I think that when he made this attack upon Mrs. Dannto, he made a serious mistake. Why? Because she was riding in an auto-taxi, remotely controlled, and the crash came about through mechanical breakdown or through deliberate manipulations at Central-control. When we find out who's responsible, we'll have a lead to this mysterious Frenchman.''

"Auto-taxi?" said Dannto, frowning. "That's funny, since she has a car and chauffeur of her own. The chauffeur is one of your men, Candleman. Why should she be in a taxi? Where was she going?"

"That is what I'd like to know. I can't ask Mrs. Dannto because Dr. Barker refused me admission. And then put her to sleep for twelve hours."

"I hope you're not doubting my professional ability," said Leif. His expression told plainly that it made no difference to him.

"Oh, no," said the Uzzite with a quick glance at Dannto. "I realize that Mrs. Dannto's health comes before anything."

"What about her escort?" asked Leif.

"He was called on the QB by an unknown person. While he was talking, Mrs. Dannto left the back way and got into a cruising auto-taxi."

"What do the machine's records show as to her destination?"

"Nothing. They were demolished in the crash. The taxi, as near as we can determine, left the road and crashed through a bridge railing. It fell thirty feet. However, Mrs. Dannto gave three different destinations during her ride. Each time she arrived, she directed the machine to another. Evidently, she was working up to her final stop by stages in an attempt at shaking off any tracker, or with the idea of jumping out and taking another taxi while the first proceeded on its way."

"Do you realize what you're saying?" demanded the Archurielite in a loud voice. "You're accusing my wife of conspiracy!"

"Not at all. Her behavior was mysterious, yes, but she will undoubtedly be able to explain it—as soon as she comes out of her sedation," he added.

"But that's not all. One of my men, who appeared at the scene of the crash shortly after it happened, told me that a little girl was run over by the taxi just before it broke the rail. My man thought she was dead, because her skull was smashed, and so he concentrated on getting Mrs. Dannto out of the taxi. When the ambulance came, he directed them to Mrs. Dannto first."

Leif said, "I suppose he had recognized her!"

"Yes, why?"

"And he didn't know the little girl?"

"No, what are you getting at?"

"Nothing important."

He was aware of Candleman's speculative stare and guessed that the Uzzite was making a mental note to ask a selfdoc just what Leif meant. Also, whether it represented a deviation from Leif's recorded behavior pattern.

"When my man returned to the bridge," continued the Uzzite, "the girl was no longer there. And the ambulance men had not picked her up. Naturally, he looked around, and he saw her being carried away by two men accompanied by two women. He called after them. They disappeared around a corner. He chased them into a subway and saw them stop behind a pillar. But when he got there, he could find no sign of them.

"He continued down the tunnel, for there was only one way they could go. At the end of the tunnel he met another of my men. This fellow swore that nobody had come through while he was there, and he'd been there for at least half an hour.

"Naturally, the latter is now being questioned. It's obvious that he must be an accomplice."

"Accomplice of what?" asked Leif.

Candleman shrugged shoulders thin as a coat-hanger.

"I don't know. But I strongly suspect they are

followers of Jacques Cuze. There was a big J.C. scratched into the cement wall close by."

"You can find those in many places in Paris," said Leif. Candleman's eyes sparked like a grindstone sharpening knives in the dark.

"I am fully aware of that. But I promise you that before the year is up, Jacques Cuze will be dead or in H."

"Why would they carry the girl off?" asked Dannto. "She couldn't get the medical care underground that she could here."

"I'm not so sure of that," said Candleman, glancing at the doctor. Leif did not condescend to reply.

"If she'd been brought here, there'd have been an investigation. And her parents would have been exposed. They preferred to let her die rather than take the chance. Anyway, she was probably dead."

"I'm surprised, Jake," said Dannto, "that you would admit that an unrealist had snatched away one of their own members from under the nose of the Uzzites."

"If there is one thing I pride myself on—one completely realist attitude—it is honesty," said Candleman. For the first time at dinner his voice bore expression. "I try to conceal nothing, in accordance with the teachings of Sigmen, real be his name, through all time."

Something that had been hidden away in Leif's brain, far down and in the darkness, suddenly began to make sense.

He leaned forward and said, "Candleman, what did these four people look like?"

The Uzzite blinked. "What do you mean?"

"Did they look—foreign? Or strange?"

"Why do you ask?"

Leif leaned back. "You answer me first."

"Shib. He said they were very blond and their

faces seemed out of proportion. The noses had huge
flaring nostrils but were high-arched. Their lips were
thick. He couldn't see the color of their eyes, of
course, being too far off, but the girl had very light
blue eyes.''

"Ah, yes," said Leif non-committally. So it *was*
the four who'd tried to detain him this morning!

"Yes, what?" asked Candleman.

"Well, if there really are Frenchmen living underground today—if this Cuze isn't entirely legendary—then they would look different from the
modern Parisian, who is a descendant of Icelanders.
Of course, there is a certain amount of French blood
in him. Not all the French perished during the
Apocalyptic Plague. The descendants of the survivors, however, were conquered and absorbed by
the invading Icelanders a century later.''

"Perhaps," said Candleman, "they did look different. I don't know. I've never seen a picture of a
pre-Apocalyptic Parisian.''

"Do you know anything of the French language?''

"No, I'm an Uzzite. If I want specialized
knowledge, I go to a specialist.

"Let me tell you," continued Candleman, leaning
forward, moving his thin hard lips like two lobster
claws, "that Jacques Cuze is no legend or myth. He
lives in the vast underground network of abandoned
subways and the even deeper ancient sewers of Paris.
From his hidden headquarters he directs his
organization. Occasionally, I'm sure, he makes ap-
pearances above ground.

"I've hunted for him from time to time. A
thousand men have been pulled from their regular
duties and sent below with hound and light and gun.
We've sealed off mile on mile of tunnel and filled
them full of gas. And killed nothing but rats.''

"Isn't it ridiculous to suppose that Frenchmen
would live centuries in those holes, keep up their

populations, retain their language and their hopes of regaining their country?'' asked Leif.

"It may look that way," replied Candleman. "But the living presence of Jacques Cuze refutes your argument."

"When did you first learn of him?"

"Several years ago we captured a Cold War Corpsman from March. Before he could bit down on the poison tooth most of them carry, one of my men shot his jaw off. When he recovered consciousness, he couldn't talk. No tongue.

"But he could write. We asked him for a confession. After a reasonable amount of resistance against questions, he agreed to write one out. He did so in March phonetics, which at one justified my suspicions that he might be a Marcher. But he only wrote two words, and then stopped. He kept pointing at them; I finally found out he wanted them pronounced. What it meant, I didn't know, but I called in a linguistics joat. He took one look, seemed puzzled, and then pronounced, aloud, the two words.

"The next I knew, I was in a hospital bed. A splinter of the prisoner's skullbone was stuck in my temple; I'd been very lucky not to have been killed at once by it.

"Later, I pieced together various reports and found out what had happened. The fellow had not only carried poison in a tooth; he had had implanted under his skull a small but powerful bomb. And this could be set off by uttering these syllables.

"He'd tricked us. His head had blown apart and killed the three men closest to him, including the linguistics man. It had also destroyed the paper.

"Fortunately, I have a very good memory. You have to in my profession, you know. I remembered the fatal words had been Jacques Cuze.

"It was after that that I began to tie up the ubiquitous J.C. with this Jacques Cuze. And then I found a paper in one of the deserted rooms in the sewers. This was brief, but it was in French. I had it translated by a linguistic joat. It was propaganda against the Haijac Union and a plea for the return of the country to those people to whom it rightfully belonged—and it named Jacques Cuze as the leader of the diehard Frenchmen, living like rats under Paris."

Dannto laughed nervously.

Candleman said, "Deride me if you want to. But I think that J.C. has launched these attacks on Mrs. Dannto. And I'm convinced that your life is in danger unless he's captured."

Chapter 11

DANNTO LISTENED TO Candleman's revelations, then put his hand over his mouth to cover a belch before he replied, "It's a pleasure to be imperiled if, in so doing, I may advance the Sturch and prepare for the temporal arrival of the Forerunner."

He paused a moment to munch upon a sandwich of antpaste and then said, "There is, of course, a certain amount of speculation among us Urielites about the meaning of the word 'temporal.'

"Some of us think that it may not necessarily mean the physical appearance of Sigmen, real be his name, upon this earthly scene. Temporal might possibly have an esoteric meaning. It might mean his appearance in some other sense. As far as that goes, he himself did not use the word 'appearance' in his *Time and the World Line*. Instead, if I remember correctly, he wrote 'arrival.' That, you'll have to concede, can mean many things besides appearance.

"It might be intended that we should take Sigmen's voyagings in time, not as chronological, but as allegorical voyagings. Thus, these people who are getting hysterical about the Timestop, and the literal reappearance of Isaac Sigmen, may be disappointed when Timestop does come.

"The truth might be that Timestop means that the Haijac Union and its Sturch may triumph over all the nations of earth, that we may conquer them, destroy their false religions and states, and set up the true Sturch. Thus, in that sense, it might be said that Sigmen has returned and that time has stopped. It would, you see, because then true stasis would arrive. There would be no more of this eternal change that is the mark of the other nations' barbarism and bestiality."

Candleman had been shifting uneasily. When Dannto paused, he broke in.

"*Abba*, I am faithful enough to you and to the Sturch you represent. There may be no doubt of that. Therefore, it hurts me to hear you speak words that border on unreal thinking. This allegorical interpretation of the Forerunner's works was once a thing that would never have come to the lips of a Jack. If it had, he would have ended up in H.

"No, don't get angry. It's true. But now, during the last twenty years or so, we literalists have seen with increasing alarm that more and more Urielites are speaking of esoteric meanings, hinting that perhaps things may not exactly be as described. I want to make it plain, right here and now, that I, and other literalists, do not like to hear such talk. It seems to us to smack of unreality. It is a sign of the degeneration of the times. It is, in fact, exactly what the Forerunner predicted. He said there would be strange doctrines and people trying to twist his words. He said to beware of them. He said such thinking would result in degenerate morals, in people turning away from reality.

"And he is right. For in the past few years we've

seen the resurrection of dancing, of women wearing immodest clothes, of lipstick and rouge, of the discarding of street veils for women. I see all these things, and I'm sick to my stomach."

"It doesn't seem to have affected your appetite," said Dannto dryly.

He spoke easily, seemingly unaffected by the Uzzite's tirade. Leif was surprised he hadn't flared out, for his words were a direct criticism of Halla Dannto. He himself, he thought, should protest, for Ava also was being scourged. But he decided that a silent contempt would hurt the man worse.

"The issue," said Dannto, "is not at all as clear as you make it. Sigmen, real be his name, was rather ambiguous in his statements as to the manner of his Timestop. I suggest you read the Works again with that thought in mind. You'll find that both literalists and allegorists have good arguments, and both can quote chapter and verse and extra-scriptural authorities to support their contentions.

"I say there is only one way to tell. Wait and see. I am certain, however, that unflinching adherence to the Sturch is the way to be sure of being rewarded on Timestop. Whatever the manner of the Forerunner's arrival, he will repay his real believers for their faith."

"Reality be his and mine," murmured Candleman with bowed head. Then, lifting it suddenly and glaring about, he said, "But there are many people who are determined to make pseudo-futures real. The Israelites and Marchers, of course; Jacques Cuze is another; and there is, I believe, still a fourth. For instance, once, during an undercity hunt, we found a crypt full of bodies. Chiseled in the stone was a single figure, a fish. It wasn't until then that we connected this fish with others that had been reported on the walls of the surface city."

"What does the fish represent?" asked Dannto.

Leif was interested, too. It was the first time he'd heard of them.

"I'll tell you," said Candleman somewhat smugly. "It's my theory that Jacques Cuze . . ."

"Oh, no, here we go again," murmured Dannto, so low that only Leif heard him.

" . . . is the religious leader of the few Christians left in Europe, all of whom are underground. The head of the Holy Timbuktu Church in Africa has promised Cuze that if he succeeds in his rebellion, he'll restore the ancient French religion there, perhaps move to Paris and make it his capital. Of course, such a cause and such a promise are hopeless, but Cuze and the Timbuktuians are unrealistic and think as such."

Leif blinked. This was new to him.

"On what facts do you base your theory?" he asked.

"On what is obvious," retorted Candleman with an irritated wave of his bony hand. "There can be no other interpretation.

"The Bantus, being Christians, still use Greek and Latin rootwords for their scientific and theological writings. The Greek word for fish is Ichthyos. The first two letters are iota and chi; I and X. These, I've been told bya linguistics expert, are the closest rendering to the Roman alphabet-letters of J. and C. I and X equal J and C, which are Jacques Cuze's initials. I stands for Ioannos, which is Greek for John. X stands for chusis, the Hellenic word for stream. Stream recalls fish, naturally, and also stands for the underground, as chusis, by a stretch of meaning, may also be understood as a subterranean river.

"It's that simple. Fish stands for IX. Ioannos Chusis; John Stream; Jacques Cuze. Thus the fish symbol is the link between the underground French patriot and the Timbuktuian church."

Leif was caught between laughter and admiration for the ability of the human mind to rationalize.

"My," marveled Dannto, "all this going on, and the only reason I found out was that Halla became a victim of these people. Perhaps. Tell me, Jake, what about the church to whom the majority of the Africans belong? The Primitives? After all, the Holy Timbuktu members reside in a comparatively small state; they don't have nearly the power or facilities for underground work that the Primitives do."

Candleman held his palms up.

"I don't really know. All I learned was from a one-hour talk with a linguistic joat, one of these jack-of-all-trades. I've not had time to study as I should. My days and nights are taken up with an immense amount of administration work and my hunt for Cuze."

"You can tell the difference if you meet them," said Leif. "The Timbuktuians will fight; the Primitives are absolute pacifists."

"I know they are," said Candleman. "They make a continent ready for plucking. If the Izzies didn't stand between them and us, we could have, overnight, two thirds of Africa. Once the Israeli Republics are overcome—and I'm confident that the return of Sigmen will see that—we'll just have to walk into the country south of the Sahara Sea to take it over."

"Passive resistance will take its toll," said Leif.

Nobody asked him to elaborate; they were too eager to discuss their own theories.

Dannto didn't think the Bantus could be much of an underground force; their skin color prevented them from activity in Europe.

Candleman replied that they could hire their work done by Cuze and Jack traitors.

"Perhaps," said Leif brightly, "J. C. could stand

for Jack Christians. There was a group once that
tried to get legal recognition within the Haijac as a
separate church from the Bantu ecclesiastical
organization, loyal to the Union and regarding the
Africans as heretics.''

"Nonsense," said Dannto. "That was a century
ago, if I remember the history I was taught in college.
They all went to H and were never heard of again.''

"If the French could hide underground for two
and a half centuries, these people could for one.''

Both the other men were scornful of the idea; it
was sailing against the wind of their theories.

"No," said Dannto, "the Forerunner, in one sense
or another, has traveled along the fields of presentation, backward and forward. He went into the
future, came back, wrote books about it, established
the Haijac and its buttress, the Sturch, and then went
off into time again. He predicted the future; all
events since then have verified his forecasts. The last
days are upon us; Timestop will soon be here.
Whether Sigmen's actual presence here will be
necessary, I don't know.

"But I do know that in his *Time and the World
Line* he mentioned, rather cryptically, the sinister
Backrunner, his antagonist, the man who will try to
undo all his good works, both in past, present, and
future. There is only that one mention, but since then
a host of apocrypha have sprung up about this
Backrunner. Many of them have since been investigated and stamped as authentic and not to be
doubted by the Sturch.

"Though Sigmen did not mention the Backrunner's name, we now know that it is that of Jude
Changer, Sigmen's contemporary and lefthanded
traveler in time.

"It is my opinion, backed by the facts, that J. C.
stands for Jude Changer.''

He held up a fat hand to stall Candleman's protest.

"I will concede that this man may be the same as Jacques Cuze, operating under that name in order to conceal his true identity. But egotist that he is, he has to let us know in a sinister manner who he really is."

The QB buzzed, and the image of an Uzzite formed in the box. His message: Thorleifsson was still missing.

That broke up the party.

Candleman jumped up, his nostrils flaring.

"Perhaps you'll believe me now, *abba*," he said to the Urielite. "The chances are that my lieutenant has been murdered while on Cuze's track. I must go at once. I'll never rest until I know what happened to him."

"Perhaps," said Leif, thinking of Thorleifsson's ashes being washed down the drains and into the sewers, "he's gone underground in pursuit of the Frenchman?"

"Nonsense, Doctor. Without notifying me?"

Candleman walked to the door of the room where Halla slept and before anybody could protest he had stepped inside. Leif jumped up and strode after him.

He found the Uzzite standing by her bedside, looking intently at her. The nurse was at the other side of the room; she had made no attempt to prevent Candleman from entering.

Leif could barely conceal his anger. "You have been told," he said in a strangled whisper, "that Mrs. Dannto was not to be disturbed. I do not want to repeat that again."

Candleman lingered over the beautiful head with its corona of flaming hair spread out on the white pillow. Then he straightened and walked out without a word. Leif felt his fists curling; he would have liked to drive them into that hard mouth.

When the Uzzite had stepped out, Leif turned to the nurse.

"You may go back to your floor," he said. "You won't be needed here."

The nurse, a dragon of eighty years, opened her mouth to protest, saw what his face meant and walked out. Leif suspected she was working for Candleman. This gave him a good excuse to dismiss her; it was irony that Candleman himself had furnished the reason.

Chapter 12

NO SOONER HAD Leif returned to the dining room than the QB buzzed again. A Urielite's form appeared in the QB. He informed his superior that the Metratron wished him to be present at an important meeting of the inner council at Montreal tomorrow. Dannto hesitated and then replied he'd be there.

"As you can see," the fat man said to Leif, "I'm very busy. This noon, an operation; tonight, I leave on the coach for Canada. I just never get time to spend with my wife."

"We'll take care of her. She can follow you tomorrow evening. Provided there are no complications."

Dannto's chin quivered with delight. He slapped Leif on the back.

"You're the best there is, Doctor."

"That's true."

Barker then QB'd his assistant and told him to prepare for a removal of a tumor from Dannto's abdomen at 1500. Also, to send up a nurse to escort the Archurielite to a room on 800, the surgical floor.

"You'll get a sedative and be bathed and dressed for the operation," said Leif.

"I was hoping I'd get to stay here longer," pouted Dannto.

"Mrs. Dannto won't be awake until 2100."

"Sigmen take it, I have to leave on the 2000 coach. Do you think I'll be able to go on it?"

"I sympathize with your predicament," said Leif, "but inasmuch as the coach doesn't accelerate fast enough to strain your incision, I can't honestly tell you to stay here overnight."

"Well, this conference is really important. I'd better go."

After he'd ushered Dannto out, Barker waited until the replacement nurse arrived for Halla. Once he'd given her her order, he went into his bedroom. Ava was sprawled out on a chair in a lace dressing gown, smoking a cigarette.

"Give me one," said Leif. "I wanted one all morning."

"I'll give you nothing," retorted Ava, "except a kick in your big head. Why did you dissect that girl instead of cremating her at once? What's up, Leif? You're not obeying the CWC's orders."

Leif put down the glow-wire with which he had lit his cigarette and began puffing on the Fruitful Times.

"Ava, I'll be frank with you. Have you considered the thoughtpicker?"

"What's that got to do with this?"

"Look. What happened when the picker went on the blink? Did we repair it?"

"No, it was carried away and another brought to replace it."

"Why?"

"I suppose because it's boobytrapped. If it's opened, it blows up. That, naturally, is to keep its secret from falling into the hands of the Jacks, if they should catch on that we're using one."

"Sure, and the trap is there to keep inquisitive Marchers out as well as Jacks. Want to know why? Because it's a loaned machine. The lenders want its structure to remain a mystery. They're afraid that the Earthmen who can manufacture such things will get too much power."

"What do you mean by Earthmen?"

"Ava, I've looked the thoughtpicker over during many lonely evenings when I'd nothing to do. There's not much to see, but from what I can make out, I'd say the thing is of alien construction and design."

Ava blinked long curling lashes.

"How did you arrive at such a startling conclusion?"

"Don't laugh. It's a feeling I get when I look at it. It just doesn't have the Terran *look*. I'll swear there's something non-human about it."

"Imagination!"

"No. Intuition."

"Is that all?"

"No. That girl, and the one I dissected, are not human."

Ava sat up.

"How do you know?"

Leif explained.

The glowing cigarette in Ava's hands shook. Leif thought Ava was more upset than necessary.

"There's something else," he said. "We know that the Haijac morals have been, by their own admission, decadent for the past hundred years. But during the last fifteen years the immorality increased. It's almost as if a catalyst from outside has been accelerating it. But what is the catalyst?

"For one thing, the CWC's been helped by this

drug that enables our agents to be injected with truth-drug and yet continue to lie. Thus, they can survive the questions before the Elohimeter and earn their gold lamechs. We've used that advantage to pass off our own men among the Jacks, men who have the inestimable opportunity to work almost unquestioned in this society and to do their damnedest damage. But where did we get that drug? We didn't invent it, I know."

"Perhaps we got it from the Jacks themselves," suggested Ava. "It wouldn't be the first time. Their sciences are so unintegrated that many inventions pass unnoticed and undeveloped."

"Yes, and that, ironically, is due to their suspicion of the giant integrating electronic 'brains' we use. Sigmen himself fostered that handicap when he warned them that the inordinate use of such machines might result in the machines 'taking over.'

"But here's the point they don't know about—we suddenly start using this drug about ten years ago. Know what I think? That it, like the thoughtpicker, is extra-terrestrial."

"And the girls are XT's who're helping us? But why should they get in the midst of it?"

"Ava, when did Jack women start using lipstick? When did the hierarchy begin drinking in private? When did we learn that there were female March agents who had an enormous influence upon the top Sturchmen?"

"You mean that these XT females initiated these changes through their influence on the hierarchy?"

"Shib. Of course, they couldn't have done it unless the Jack women were ripe for such a thing. That it was done so easily proves they were. And, Ava, who first called the council of Urielites to debate a certain scriptual passage? And who influenced the council to interpret it in such a way that women could use cosmetics?"

"Dannto. At Halla's urgings. There's one inconsistency. How did these girls come to influence them in the first place? Time was when they'd be hauled off to H without a second thought just for suggesting the changes."

"That," said Leif slowly, "is what I intend finding out. They must have something that is really powerful, almost magical. And I intend to find out what it is."

He went to a cabinet and pulled out a bottle of alcohol, which he mixed with a purplish fluid.

Leif said, "By the way, not to get off the subject, I think Shant's in love with you. Those sheep eyes!"

Ava exploded. "Every time we're alone he makes a pass at me. Him and his big hypocritical mealymouth when others are around—and then those sticky little paws of his when nobody's looking! The next time, I'm breaking his teeth. Orders or no orders."

"Now look who's disobeying. You're a poor soldier. You know I told you to string him along. He's a good source of information, and we might want to use his lust for you to get us out of a spot."

"Well, I can't let him get *too* close."

"Heh, heh!" Leif threw a half-glass down his throat. "Good thing this stuff smells like ether. Otherwise I'd shock the nurses. I'm not too sure it *isn't* ether."

He shuddered and then filled another glass.

"Here's the setup, Ava. I cut Dannto's tumor out at 1500. Candleman will be watching the operation through the QB. You set it to break down at 1515. Peter Sorn will get the blame. We'll send an anonymous accusation later. Whether that'll be enough to send him to H, I don't know. The tech shortage is getting so acute that the Uzzites, inflexible though they are, have not been nearly so eager to ship them off as they were when we first started this. However, a few more 'sabotages' like that, and they won't be able to overlook Sorn."

"Too bad about Peter," said Ava. "He's one of the few people in this hospital I can stand. Why can't we fix up sneaky old Gunnarsson?"

"You know why. Because he's not the tech Sorn is. The Jacks won't miss him as much."

"I'd like to send that little lecher Shant down. When are we going to start on him?"

"Ah, ah, let's leave personalities out of this."

"Do you know Leif, I still can't see why Jackasses haven't tumbled to our technique? Are they really that stupid?"

"No, you mustn't make that mistake. Their I.Q., I imagine, is about the same average as that of the people of other nations. You see, Ava, you hear much about the high intelligence of the Izzies because they're partly descended from the citizens of Israeli, one of the few organized and undecimated countries left after the Apocalyptic War. The theory goes that those people then living represented a group whose history included so many thousands of years of oppression, of persecution, of weeding out, that only the mentally alert survived. When the overcrowded little country was presented with lands where only a few unorganized, dazed survivors dwelt, it almost literally exploded. In an amazingly short time colonies ringed the Mediterranean; these grew, fed by families that normally included a dozen children. Morality rates were low, and newly-invented rejuvenation techniques kept parents propagating far into their nineties.

"There were quite a few people living in the lands to which these colonists came. They were ineffective because they were widely separated and because they'd reverted to a primitive agricultural society. But they were treated well, because the Israeli constitutions guaranteed them full rights. Nevertheless, inevitably, they were absorbed; their genes, their languages, their customs. And their descendants were none the worse off. I'd say they benefited.

"Remarkably enough, the Icelanders could make the same claim. None but the strong and the clever survived the extremely harsh environment of Iceland from the first colonization in the tenth century A.D. up through the eighteenth century A.D. And their descendants, like those of the Israelites, were keen and independent.

"So, too, the Hawaiians, perhaps the most mixed in race of all people, a melting pot of Mongolian, Polynesian, Caucasian, and, in short, just about anything you cared to name. It was this heterosis, perhaps, that accounted for the fact that the Hawaiians spread faster and further than any of the others, so that they repopulated the Americas, Japan, China and eastern Siberia."

Ava spoke first. "Thank *you*, Professor Barker. Then why did the democratic, high-I.Q. Icelanders and Hawaiians become what amounted to slaves?"

"Their present subservience should be a warning to all. We, and the Israelites, who pride outselves on our democratic traditions, might easily have gone the same way. And would have, if it had not been for several great men among the early Israeli colonists of the Mediterranean countries who gave their lives that the constitutions might be preserved.

"What happened in the Haijac was that this man Sigman came along when there was a great deal of strife and unrest. Also, this was the age of religious revival, if you'll remember, Everywhere, all over the world, a spirit long thought dead arose and strode across continents. Sigmen, the founder of an obscure and crackpot psuedo-Christian cult, rose to glory on the crest of the wave. He had what the other prophets lacked—a pseudo-scientific explanation for what had been considered spiritual phenomena. Now, he claimed, it was no longer a matter of faith; it was facing the facts. He presented his distortions of the theories of Dunne on time. He explained, to his disciples' satisfaction, anyway, all historical and religious events in the light of the neo-Dunnology.

"Moreover, after he'd seized power, he kept it personally for several hundred years, a thing no other politician or conqueror had ever been able to do, because they didn't have longevity drugs. Using the usual brutal means, he set up a state in which the citizens, for their own good, of course, underwent a constant and intimate security. The guardian-angel-pro-tempore system, plus systematic sublimation of normal human drives, resulted in what you see today.

"In addition to that, he utilized the tremendous prestige of the Israeli Republics to add to his own. He took the admiration of his own subjects for the Mediterranean power and perverted it. He wrote his Western Talmud, adopted the Hebrew language as the theological and scientific language, and, in short, made a mockery and a travesty of us for his own purposes. And, probably, all in good faith."

Ava deliberately yawned and said, "Thanks for the history lesson, Teacher. Why don't you tell me something I don't know?"

Annoyed, Leif said, "I will. I've a criticism, Ava, that might not seem much to you, but it might be one of the little things that'll give us away. Please try to restrain your disgust when you're eating certain foods. I'm afraid it's going to be noticed."

"But Leif, mouse fricassee! And ant jelly! Every time I sit down to eat, I see nothing but unclean food!"

"It's part of your duty."

"If I'd known that, I'd never have volunteered for this. I don't mind skirting death, a dozen times a day. But the food!"

Leif guffawed.

Ava said, 'Laugh, you *kelev*. You're a shame to

your fathers and your grandfathers.''

"They ate the same things I did. Do you know, it's rare to find an orthodox Judaist in March. Why did your mother and father flee Sephardia and take refuge in March? It couldn't have been the strict orthodoxy of Sephardia because you're orthodox. Was your father a political liberal? Or a criminal?''

Leif referred to the Republic of Sephardia, which once had been called Spain and Portugal.

"Why did my parents leave Sephardia?" said Ava. "Because of love. My father met my mother while on a business trip to Cairo. She was a beauty with the biggest darkest eyes you ever saw. She and my father fell passionately in love. And that was a problem not easy to solve. Father was strict orthodox, and mother was an agnostic. They're very liberal in Khem, you know. Unlike Sephardia, Khem has religious freedom.

"Both families objected to the marriage. Father and mother married anyway and settled down in Khem in the city of Aswan. But my mother's family, despite its professed liberalism, persecuted my father by ruining his business and even accused him of being a spy from Sephardia. For all I know, he may have been. Sephardia and Khem had both declared independence of the Israeli Confederation, you know, and were on the point of going to war with each other.

"So my parents went to March, and I was born in Afenyaw, ancient Avignon, shortly after they arrived. It's not been too easy for me in March, and it's been worse since I was sent here as a CWC-man. Of course, I've been released from all obligations to practice dietary restrictions because I am posing as a Jack. But I can't help how my nervous system reacts. My stomach threatens to upheave every day at mealtime.''

"Well," said Leif, "you'll get no sympathy from

me on the food. I respect religious beliefs . . ."

"Sure you do," mocked Ava.

". . . but this business about taboo dishes is beyond my comprehension."

"Let's not get into that weary and fruitless discussion again," said Ava. "I'll stick to my beliefs; you're stuck with yours."

Leif smiled and said, "So you got your big dark eyes from your mother? You charmer, you. Well, I think I'll look in on Halla. Oh, before I go, I'm putting the 'picker on Dannto during the operation. Will you change the beeper to the kymo? I'll read it later."

Ava nodded.

Leif hesitated and said, "I wish now I'd kept Candleman out of surgery. His mind would be more profitable to pick than the Archurielite's."

"I could train it on him," said Ava. "No, the walls are lined with stoprays, aren't they?"

"Yes. Well, we'll get him soon as possible. He makes me uneasy. I think he's suspicious of me."

"It's your face, darling."

"Well, it's the one you married, honey. Come here, give me a kiss."

"You'd look better with your front teeth missing," and Ava's black eyes glittered.

"Exit laughing," said Leif, and did.

He entered Halla's room.

"You may go to the kitchen and eat," he said to the nurse.

After she had left, he sat down by the bedside and began talking to the sleeping beauty. From the beginning, he'd had this session in mind, so he'd given her not an ordinary sleeping potion but a lotus pill. The semi-hypnotic drug would open the way for him to probe her subconscious.

He hadn't gotten far into his questions about her past when he found that a posthypnotic block had been installed. She simply would not answer anything that contradicted the fictitious personality of her sister.

If he had cared to or had available the time needed, he could have broken down the barrier. But as he did not have days on end or a host of drugs handy, he gave up.

He rose and went to surgery. There he stripped off his clothes, was soaped and showered, but did not get the expected blast of warm air to dry him. He was forced to call a maintenance man and then, not to lose time, to dry himself off with towels. Afterwards he put on a plastic gown, mask, pants and shoes, which would be discarded after the operation. He put on his surgeon's gloves, stood for a moment bathing in microbe-killing radiation, and then entered the operating room.

Dannto was lying upon a table. As the Archurielite had taken only a local, he was looking around him with bright eyes at the various plastic containers above him and the tubes that ran from them to the needles in his arms.

Though pale, he twisted his fat face into a smile. Leif held up a curved thumb and forefinger in a gesture a thousand years old and then checked on the routine. Ava, he noticed, was busy in the corner unscrewing the leads to the picker's beeper and connecting them to the stylo. Nobody questioned what Ava was doing; Sigur, the eegie man, had gone home.

Dannto did not object when Leif asked him if it were all right if the eegie helmet were placed over his head during the operation. Leif explained that he had many records so far of the lower classes, but none of exceptionally intelligent men. Dannto tried to hide his pleasure. It would be quite all right. Anything in the interests of science.

Actually, it was not at all necessary that the helmet

come in contact with the subject's head. It could pick up the brain waves of a selected person at a considerable distance on its tight beam. But Leif wanted to make things look as authentic as possible; there was no use taking a chance on anybody's recognizing its unorthodoxy.

While he operated, Leif talked to the Urielite, first taking the precaution of asking him to keep silent unless told to talk. He chattered amusingly of this and that inconsequence, like any good doctor trying to keep his patient's mind off the knife.

Now and then he inserted a statement that he hoped would send Dannto thinking along certain lines. He expected, if the train of thought continued, to extract valuable information from the waves inked upon the kymo slowly turning in the corner.

He could not keep from thinking of the girl in the penthouse bedroom, asleep, her long, loose and wavy hair piling out gloriously upon the pillow. The head would be turned aside, the profile against the auburn hair, a cameo of vibrant flesh against gleaming tresses.

And she, he thought, belonged to the mass of dough that he was now paring away. His hand shook. He steadied it; though he controlled himself, he could not help the desire that seized it. What if he were to slip? To make a wrong cut?

Well, what about it? Candleman would investigate. Routinely, of course. And there would be no telling what that bloodhound would sniff out. Perhaps enough to undo all the work fo the CWC for the past ten years. No, he certainly couldn't do it. He'd allowed himself enough disobedience this morning when he'd dissected Mrs. Dannto. Moreover, Ava had left the 'picker and was watching him. Ava's trained eye would grasp the deliberately false move, the premeditated, fatal slip. And, knowing, Ava's duty would be to inform Marsey that he had disobeyed orders. That would mean his recall, or, more probably, a drumhead courtmartial and execution in Paris. It was too risky to smuggle a man like him across the border; it would not be worth taking the chance. So somebody he didn't know was in the Corps would step up to him one night, and stab him and carve J.C. across his forehead and thus kill two birds with one cut, inspiring terror among the Jacks and squelching any suspicion the Sturch might have had that he was an Izzie or March agent. Very clever and economical.

Thinking thus, the doctor made the correct motions and in due time removed a tumor which would never have grown if Dannto had not taken a certain medicine prescribed by Leif.

"This will do good," he'd said, not saying for whom. The Urielite had swallowed it in the faith that his stomach aches would vanish. So they had, but he had planted the seed of a larger one.

The good doctor now plucked the fruit, then filled the cavity with a quivering mass of jelly. The shapeless mass would at once lock its 'blueprint' electromagnetic field to the injured cells. The amino-acid and CH contents would form new cells. In a surprisingly short time, the tissues would be as good as new.

This particular jelly was somewhat different, however. Part of it consisted of a substance whose ingredients, unmixed, were harmless. If a shortwave of a certain frequency, sent at certain close intervals, struck the substance, the substance mixed, formed a violent poison, and sent the owner thereof, into a quick and fatal convulsion. Leif stepped back while the nurses finished up the sterilizing and other lesser tasks. "How do you feel?"

Dannto, pale as a toadstool, said, "Never bothered me a bit."

He pointed to the mirror overhead. "It's quite an

experience, looking into yourself.''

"Very few people do," said Leif without humor, and was not disappointed when Dannto failed to comprehend.

"You may dress in that room, *abba*," said a nurse.

Dannto waddled towards the indicated door, but before he reached it, he was halted by Candleman's voice. The Uzzite had burst in through another entrance.

"Time's end!" he swore. "Who's responsible for the QB here?"

"Peter Sorn is," said Leif. "Why?"

"That's the same fellow I had questioned about room 113, isn't he?"

He whirled and stalked off, leaving the others standing staring at him. When Dannto asked Leif what the matter was, Leif shrugged. Nevertheless, he felt slightly sick.

Chapter 13

AFTER THE ROOM had been cleaned up, and the nurses and Ava had left, Leif returned to the operating room to see what the thoughtpicker had recorded during the operation. The thoughtpicker was a machine mounted upon a three-wheeled carriage. Its bulk was enclosed in a shining seamless eternalloy sphere set upon the top of the rest of the machinery.

Sigur, the assistant eegieman, had been curious. It had taken only a word from his superior to make that curiosity voiceless; Leif had hinted that it was an invention of great importance and that the Sturch would frown upon any noising about of its presence. This followed the pattern. Sigur swore that he'd be as silent as expected.

Leif removed the kymographs, took them to a table, spread them out, and began studying. He paid no attention to the upper lines; those were the conventional waves. The bottom line, inked by the newly hooked-in-stylus, took all his concentration for the next hour. He read the peaks and plunging valleys swiftly, for his training had been thorough, and his experience had given him vast familiarity with them. Dannto's thoughts were spread out before him; the things he expected no man would ever know.

At the end of the hour, Leif sighed.

Thoughts were not what one expected. When Leif had been introduced to the thoughtpicker in the CWC's *sanctum sanctorum*, he'd been thrilled. Read a man's mind? Train a narrow beam on an unsuspecting skull, pick up and amplify the very weak 'semantic' waves, interpret their climbs and slides, and know all his secrets?

Be God?

Hah!

First, the young student had learned that beneath the well-known alpha, beta, gamma, eta, theta, and iota waves were the sigma or semantic. These almost indetectable eruptions could be correlated by the trained eye to the spoken word. With some training the learner could slide across the graph a bar with a rectangular hole in its center, blocking off each unit and seeing it as such, not as just another continuation of the jagged lines.

Later, after hard study, the time came when the eye could run down the dales and leap over the hills inked upon the paper and know what it was reading.

Could it?

Not entirely. Leif had found out that if a man thought out a sentence you asked him to cerebrate, the 'picker could reproduce the words. But that was all. It couldn't give you the emotions or the thousand other events that went with the stylo-ized waves. It couldn't portray the inner sensations: the feelings of repulsion, annoyance, lust, love, or boredom. It couldn't tell you a man was hungry or describe his reactions to a beautiful woman walking down the street.

If a man thought, *Forerunner, I'm hungry enough*

to eat the hind end of a skunk, or *Boy, what a classy chassis!*, and his tongue repeated sublingually those stirring words, the waves broadcast by his brain could be caught and kymoed.

What if he stood silent upon a peak in Darien?

You, the god with the mindreader, suddenly found yourself scanning a new tongue, the undecipherable hieroglyphics called, technically, static.

Leif had been taught at the CWC College that the waves which could be correlated with definite spoken syllables were to be known as logikons or word-images.

Where, the young Dr. Baker had thought, were the other ikons?

There were none. None, at least, that could be picked up by the machine.

This was not true telepathy, the mindreading conceived by science-fiction writers and scientists.

This brainskimming was a travesty on that concept, a mockery of man's hopes.

You read a sentence and then came to a blank. Or found a word cut off in half. You knew that these pauses were full of 'thinking.' But words were not all that were used in thinking. And, unfortunately, words were all you could interpret. Great seas of non-intelligibility surrounded little islands of knowableness.

Leif, after studying the 'picker for ten years, concluded that a new machine needed to be built.

It must be capable of detecting and interpreting *all* the impulses sent by the muscles, the nerves, the glands, and, in short, the total of organs. Suppose you could get the wave-image of bodily posture and the internal sensations integrated thereto? What would you have? The kinesthetikon?

That, of course, would be changing from second to second. Image stepping on image's heels.

Then you'd have to add to that the feelings engen-

dered by reception of beauty or ugliness from outside
the skin or inside: the sight of a sunset, the taste of a
thick and tender steak. These multiplex images would
form a whole: the esthetikon.

Integrate all the incredibly complicated phenomena of signs and symbols and the reactions to them,
the weaving of ikons, and what would you get?

The semantikon: the meaning-image.

And how would you know what this image looked
like?

It wasn't as difficult to find as you might think.

Meaning, or another word for it, value, was *what
you did*. Action and reaction made up the moving
ikon. Idols rose and fell, and their birth, power, and
toppling were you as you passed through frames of
time and space and perhaps other frames that some
do not recognize and others do, even if only faintly.

So, thought Leif, if that were true, where would
you get a machine to show you the transient ikons
and the one big image they formed? And if you had
the machine, how would you present the semantikon
to the reader so he might see that multiltude of wave
pictures in one word, in one *symbol?* How would you
hurl that symbol long distances for instant communication? What could do that? What could receive
it?

The question was, he suspected, wrongly phrased.
It wasn't *what*. It was *who*.

The answer was obvious. He'd seen just such a
machine that very morning. Four machines. As a
result of his busyness—or stupidity—he'd probably
lost forever his chance to study one.

Sighing, he bent over Dannto's record. As he'd expected, there was nothing unusual here. The Sandalphon was a man. A man didn't differ from his
fellows as much as he liked to think. No matter how
high his position or his deeds, his morals or his I.Q.,

he concerned himself with much the same things as the fellow next door and had much the same reactions.

Dannto was scared of dying on the table under Leif's knife, even though he had great confidence in his ability. There was one main suspicion; what if some of his inferiors had managed to bribe the doctor into slipping with the blade?

That was rejected as unworthy. Barker was a fine doctor and a pleasant fellow, even if his conversation did sometimes border on unreality. He was, in a way, a very modest person. Look how he'd snatched Halla from the hands of the angel of death. Yet he'd pooh-poohed her wounds in order to save him, Dannto, his temporal master, grief and worry.

Here Leif read snatches of thoughts, interspersed by stretches or 'static,' the technical term for uninterpretable waves. The gist was the Dannto had first seen Halla ten years ago when she'd applied for a job. She had been the secretary of the Metatron of Northern Asia. When that man had been killed in an accident (ha, thought Leif, the good old murderous CWC again) she'd applied for transfer to Paris and, rare event, gotten it.

Here there were flashes of something; a partial phrase of 'the first time I saw her unveiled'; followed by a cavalry charge of lancelike peaks, interpreted by Leif as emotion. Then there was a sentence of approval on high heels, lipstick and discard of veils, although they'd been for some years a more or less established fact.

A pause. There were many pauses, as the brain, like other organs of the body, rested between beats. Then, out of nowhere, speculations about Candleman; how he'd raved on hearing the pronouncements of the council of Rek; denounced the increasing degeneration of the Haijac as signified by the daring dresses of women and the increased use of alcohol and the unconcerns of those who ought to stamp such things out.

An interjected and irrelevant thought about asking Barker for a stronger laxative; then the tag end of a joke he'd heard the other day; then the recent offer of a bribe by the director of a spaceship contruction department, and his hesitation over whether or not it might be a trap, devised by his inferiors to displace him and his final conclusion that he would denounce the would-be briber. He didn't need the money, anyway.

Here and there hopped his thought, a kangaroo going no place in particular, stopping to nibble at this and that tender bush.

Candleman entered again, like a draft in a haunted house, drifting in through a broken window and rippling the neck with the thought that perhaps a ghost was behind him. The Uzzite's long hunt for Jacques Cuze was becoming a problem, interfering with his efficiency on other matters. Candleman's keen and hot pursuit of the underground character was almost metaphysical, he had so many complicated theories as to *who* Cuze was, *where* he was, *what* he was doing now and going to do next. More static: probably a picture of Candleman in some pose or other; then, verification, the sub-vocalized English phrase "axenosed bloodhound," applied to Candleman.

Static. A wonder if he should diet. Halla had made some teasing references to his paunch getting in the way. A dwelling on his past jealousies over this and that man who'd been interested in her; there were so many. Some he'd transferred; others demoted; about three of the most tiresome he'd sent to H. Not that he distrusted Halla, but then you never know. Remember Sigmen's warnings to believe only what you saw a woman doing and then check on that. Static. That old bastard Sigmen must have hated women for some reason. Was he . . . static . . . forgive me, good Forerunner, for these unreal thoughts. I am weak and these awful . . . offal . . . heh, heh . . . ideas sometimes seize me . . . sent, no doubt, by the sinister Backrunner, who can implant unreality by telepathy. J.C.? J.C.? That fool, Candleman, and his Jacques Cuze. Jude Changer is the man behind that, you can bet . . . static . . . gap.

I forgot to get my fingernails cleaned . . . must have that new manicurist Rahab . . . significant name . . . do them. Halla will be too weak for a while . . . no, shameful . . . shameful . . . wonder how Leif's making out with his secretary? Rachel's pretty, but I'll bet cold, an icicle on two legs . . . like so many women . . . Halla only *real* women ever had . . . what colleagues think if knew that . . . Sigmen says sex ought to be repressed . . . make more amenable citizens . . . shib . . . shib . . . but what about hierarchy . . . should they be same as citizens? Better than . . . Halla only woman knows how give . . . Sigmen, what if I die while thinking these unreal thoughts . . . forgive . . . the old Backrunner in me . . .

So that's how I . . . I . . . I . . . I . . . I . . . look inside me. Nest of worms . . . Leif good man . . . won't make mistake . . . hope . . . hope . . . ah, to die, never see Halla again . . . she go to another man . . . Sigmen! Rather she died . . . static . . .

And then a long and sustained vision of what would happen after the Timestop. Leif could not see the images; he had to piece them together from stray words. Sigmen would make the pseudo-worlds real and give each and every one of his faithful followers an entire universe to rule. Imagine your own Cosmos . . . get it on a platter . . . step through a door, leave this world . . . all hail, Emperor of Infinity,

Sovereign of Eternity . . . what is your will? will?
will? and so the echo bounced down the resonant
chambers of the mind.

Leif could imagine the orgy burning through the
forest of neurons, he'd seen enough into the minds of
other men to guess that. He wasn't particularly
disgusted; what did make him recoil a trifle was the
hypocrisy.

Leif dutifully read the rest of the kymo. Most of it
was the usual Augean flood; he did smile when he
came across more irrepressible doubts about the
beliefs of the Sturch, and Dannto's thought that he
might have been wasting his time so rigorously
following a falsehood. Then more anguished cerebral
bellows of repentance and demands for forgiveness,
all quite stylized, doubt here being put upon a for-
malistic religious basis. Then came the concluding
prayer that he be given the zealous fanatical certainty
and unswerving faith of Candleman. But not, dear
Sigmen, the one-dimensional mind that went with
them.

"Amen," said Leif and dropped the graph into the
incinerator.

Chapter 14

INSERTING FRESH PAPER in the kymo, Lief turned to go. He paused, startled, for a man in a white orderly's smock stood by the door. He had a pale skin, red hair, blue eyes and a high-arched, flare-nostriled nose.

"*Shalom*, Jim Crew," said Leif.

"*Shalom*," said Crew.

"Do you still want the same thing?" Leif asked.

"You know I do, Dr. Barker. We could have let our child die long ago. But we love her, and so we've been . . . holding her hand . . . because we know that there are some things we can't do."

"There are other surgeons in this city. Why come to me?"

He turned to the 'picker and flicked on the toggle. Then he turned the helmet until the dial registered impact with cerebral waves. He turned another dial so the helmet, whose inner surface was the receiver, would turn, following the source of radiation as a flower focuses upon the sun. Nor, if Leif's waves crossed the beam, would it be confused, for it was set for Crew's individual pattern.

Crew smiled.

"You need not do that, Doctor. Look at the graph."

Leif saw nothing but static. He turned to face Crew.

"You are deliberately creating that?"

"Yes. You can, too, with instruction. And with the will."

"You still haven't answered my question. Why come to me?"

Crew stepped closer, walking upon his toes, turned slightly inward.

He looked earnestly into the surgeon's face.

"There are several other doctors who could help our child. But these would all inform the Uzzites. You will not."

"Why not?"

"Because, first and least important, you would fear we would write a note to Candleman and tell him that you are not Leif Barker, but Lev Baruch; that you are the leader of the most important movement of the CWC; that many Marchers are wearing the lamech because of a drug that enables them to pass the Elohimeter; that you know what Jacques Cuze means.

"That alone would make you come with us. But we won't use such means, Dr. Barker. We would let our child die rather than use force, even mental force. Such violence could only recoil upon us. You will come because it is not your nature to allow a child to die."

"You're very sure of yourself," said Leif with some difficulty. "If you won't use coercion, why call on me at all? You must know that by doing so I'm not only exposing myself to the Jacks, but my own people as well. If they hear of it, they'll be gunning for me."

"I notice you said doing, not *if* you do. But I'll answer you. We're appealing to your humanity. Those other issues don't matter. They are based upon bloodshed, murder, treachery, hate."

"True," said Leif. "But a man must defend himself."

"The best defense is none."

"We won't get far exchanging platitudes like two wise owls hooting at each other. What kind of surgical equipment do you have?"

Jim Crew gestured helplessly. "We don't use medicines. The little equipment we do have, we borrowed from our neighbors, the Timbuktumen."

"Very well. Describe the child's injury."

As Jim Crew closed his eyes and gave a very accurate word-picture, Leif ticked off what he would need. He couldn't carry too bulky a load; he would have to improvise.

He had rationalized that he was doing the CWC a service by contacting this unknown underground and thus finding out what the Bantus were doing. Though the Africans were a negligible military power, the Free State of March might like to use them at some time.

Barker knew he was rationalizing; the service would consider his actions material for court-martial. But man must rationalize, even when he knows it.

While he was collecting the materials from the Pharm in the adjoining room, Leif said. "Where did you Banties get that depigmentizing technique?"

"Curiously enough, it's the invention of a Jack convert," said Jim Crew. "The full details for extracting or depositing pigment have been lying for fifty years in the files of the professional journal for kerationologists. It, like many others that could be utilized, has sunk into the dust of libraries. The joat who read it never realized its possibilities. And the inventor himself escaped to Capetown."

Without asking permission, Leif tilted the man's head so the light fell on the desired angle of the nose. "You should have had me put in the artificial arch," he said. "I'd not have left any surgical signs there or on your lips."

"The scar appeared after we were depigmentized. The process seemed to bring them out."

Leif grunted, unimpressed. "Let's go."

They took the service car and left separately, by the hospital's rear, through the personnel's door. The Uzzite on guard there flashed his light. Leif showed his lamech; Jim Crew, his ID.

"Where did you get the uniform and the card?" asked Leif, as they climbed into his runabout.

"My brother used to work here," said the African. "We knew we would have a use for such things some day."

Leif started the motor and turned on the headlights. "How did you four get in here this morning? I know the Uzzites weren't watching then, but just the same it's very difficult to pass the regular gapts."

"We have lovers."

"Ah! And why did all of you have to come! Why not one?"

"Together we are more than just four or just one."

"The whole is greater than the parts?"

"Something like that."

Jim Crew watched Leif drive for a while and then said, "How do you know where we are going?"

Leif blinked and said, "I don't know. Rather, I just *knew*."

He paused. "I had the *feeling* of my destination."

He struck the wheel with his left fist. "It's gone now!"

"I shouldn't have said anything," purred Jim Crew. "You are like a child who knows something until it is pointed out by an ignorant adult that he can't possibly know. Then, of course, he no longer knows."

"Well, where do we go?"

Crew pointed. Leif turned the wheel in the direction indicated.

After a while, the Bantu said, "We are being followed."

"I might have known we couldn't get away with it," said Leif. He looked at the rear-view mirror but could not see any cars.

"Where are they?"

"Around the corner."

"Listen," said Leif. "If they catch us, I'm protecting myself. I'm claiming that you forced me at gun's point to go with you to operate on your daughter."

Jim Crew shivered and said, "I don't like being accused of violence, but just as you say. Only, I think you'd better kill me. Otherwise, they'll drug the truth out of me."

He pressed the accelerator to the floor. The most the car could do was forty kph; the Uzzite's car would be capable of twice that much.

"They can catch us, but they'll probably let us go to our destination," said Leif. "I'd like it if we could abandon this car and make our way on foot."

"Set the controls for auto," suggested Jim. "After we turn the next corner. We can get out and go down that subway entrance."

As they rounded the huge block of a building, Leif slammed on the brakes. They slowed to ten, he set the dials, and then he and Crew jumped out. Neither fell. They struck the ground running and continued unchecked into the subway entrance.

"This won't fool them long," said Leif. "They'll be back shortly, and they may have radioed the Uzzites at the gates to watch for us."

Jim Crew ran down the granite-looking plastic steps. He did not turn to the right, which led to the platforms, but the other way, which ran to a large room housing various concession and comfort stations.

They had to force their way through crowds. This was the hour when many were on their way home from work; besides, the stations were always thronged with Paris' overpopulation.

Naturally, there would be many gapts and Uzzites among them who would, if outcry arose, seize them. But Leif had thrown his coat back so his lamech showed. The sight of it was a trumpet blast; everybody stepped to one side.

When they went into the indicated lane, Leif appreciated the Jack modesty which he'd once mocked. Heirs of the long dead Parisians, the present occupants had rejected the Gallic earthiness and substituted their own code of bashfulness. This included many cubicles with swinging doors that reached from ceiling to floor to insure privacy.

As the gapt turned away at a secret signal, both men entered a cubicle. Leif notice the J. C. scratched on the door. He raised his brows, for it was his first indication that the Banties also had utilized that sign and symbol. It was, he thought, natural, for it could easily represent their Lord and Master and also helped to confuse them with the legendary Frenchman, perhaps to disguise altogether their presence in Paris.

The Banties were using the Marchers. Could the Marchers use them?

When the two had crowded into the closet, Jim

said, "Don't snap the lock. That would be the surest thing to lead the Uzzites to us."

"Give me credit for brains."

Jim didn't reply. Reaching up as far as he could, he pressed against a square in the pattern stamped into the plastic pseudo-marble.

"Left hand corner, seven down for the Seven Deadly Sins, three across for the Trinity that wipes them out," said Jim Crew. "It doesn't work unless you press rapidly seven times, pause three seconds, and then press three more."

The section slid backwards and then to one side. Jim Crew stepped in and turned around to beckon Leif. Smiling, he went through. The Bantie pushed the rectangle back into place.

Down they went on a spiral. The surgeon counted three hundred steps, easily enough to take them below the level of the present-day subways. They must be getting close to the ancient subways or the pre-Apocalyptic sewers.

Presently the Bantie warned his blind follower to stop; they were coming to a door. Leif couldn't see what moves the man was making, but his hand was seized and placed upon a lever.

"It's to the right, halfway down," said Crew.

"Thanks. But we surely won't be coming back the same way?"

"No. It's a good thing to know, though, if you have to take this route again."

"You're very open about these things."

"We trust you."

Leif wondered if the fellow ever used anything but the editorial plural. He didn't seem to have an ego of his own.

They stepped out into what must have been a long tunnel with a high roof, for their whispers and the shuffle of their feet came back to them hollow and magnified.

"What about using a light?" asked Leif.

Jim Crew seemed surprised. "What? Oh yes, if it will make you feel any better. But you can trust that we won't fall—we *know* these places."

Somehow, Leif felt reproached. His hand dropped from his coat pocket, his flashlight untouched. Nevertheless, he would have liked to get a glimpse of the legendary underground of Paris.

They stopped on the lip of a ledge of concrete. Crew let himself down over it and helped Leif. Before they'd gone a few steps, Leif halted to feel around on the floor.

"There used to be iron tracks here," he said.

"Yes, this was, at one time, the top-level track for the subway. But as years went by and the city kept on building up and up, it became one of the lowest. Then, when Paris was C-bombed, these tunnels became sealed off by a fused silicon sheet. A new Paris was built upon it. But come. We've a long way to go. And Anadi is getting further away from her fathers and mothers; we know that strength is draining from our hands faster and faster."

"It would be very sociable of you if you would explain what you're talking about."

"We . . . *ssh!*"

Jim Crew dropped so suddenly that Leif bumped into him. Instantly, Leif pulled his flash and automatic out, one in each hand. The Bantu grabbed his shoulder and ran his hand down the doctor's arm, feeling for his hand.

"Put those away," was his whispered rebuke.

A voice whispered from the darkness, very near, very low, and yet so close that Leif could have sworn the breath fanned his cheek.

"Jim Crew, Leif Barker."

Chills raked down his back. He raised his flash to center it upon the owner of the voice. Before he could press the button to turn it on, he felt the tube snatched from his fingers.

"Damn it, Crew,!" he bellowed, forgetting all caution. "Give that back!"

"May the Lord forgive you," whispered the Bantu. "I didn't do that."

"There's something funny about this," replied Leif, automatically lowering his voice. "What're you trying to pull on me? *That was the voice of Halla Dannto!*"

"Which one?" husked Crew.

"What do you mean? I've only heard the second . . ."

He trailed off into a sigh as the full significance seized his throat.

Hoarsely, he said, "Come on, give. *Who* is that?"

Jim Crew moved close to Leif. His shudders ran down his arm and shook Leif's. Suddenly a hand, presumably the Bantu's, reached out from the dark and traced two perpendicular lines across the surgeon's forehead.

"In that sign, save us," whispered the African.

Leif felt like echoing him. He opened his mouth to ask another question, and a long, thin, and hard object was thrust into it. He bit down on it, went to spit it out, and stopped, for it was his flashlight. At the same time, somebody tittered.

The next moment, disregarding Crew's warning cry, he turned it on.

He wished he hadn't.

It *was* Halla Dannto standing in the darkness.

Not the woman in the bed in 113.

The woman who had submitted to his knife. The woman upon the marble slab. After he had dissected her.

He cried out and then, trying to control himself, bit down upon his lower lip so hard that the blood flowed and left salt in his mouth.

The cone of light wavered as his hand shook, but it showed distinctly the scalp rolled back like an orange peeling, the gaping chest and abdomen.

"What is that?" he snarled.

Fury was replacing panic.

The Bantu gripped his arm and said, "Try hard. Try hard to see *through* her, see who's *behind* her."

Leif didn't understand him. Nevertheless, he made an effort to stare the thing down, to look, as Crew suggested, through her. It was almost impossible to do. She frightened and nauseated him; facing her was like facing his own conscience.

The floodtide of anger helped him. He couldn't keep out the idea that perhaps the Bantu and an accomplice were playing a trick of some kind on him. Reason told him otherwise. Crew had not known beforehand that they were coming down this way. Besides, what could be the purpose of such a fraud?

That thing was no masquerade; it was real!

Chapter 15

LEIF STEPPED FORWARD, holding the beam steady as he did so. The figure wavered, became slightly out-of-focus, melted. For a second Leif could see through it and glimpsed the face of a man. It was one like Crew's: very pale, thick-lipped, with a nose with broad nostrils and high arch. The mouth was open and drooling; the eyes were closed tightly as if the light hurt them.

"That's far enough," said Jim Crew. "Don't make him angry! Leave him alone. He won't hurt us. That is, if you turn the light off, he won't."

The doctor hated to relinquish the beam, for he felt helpless in the dark with a *thing* like that close, a thing that obviously could move in the night of tunnel as confidently as he could at high noon on an open street. So urgent was his companion's voice, so compelling, he obeyed.

Jim Crew sighed, "Ah!" He said, "Let's go. I don't think he'll follow."

His hand pulled Leif's. The latter, his spine tingling at the idea of a knife sinking in from behind, let himself be guided down the crumbling tracks. When they'd traveled exactly five hundred steps, when he no longer felt that other feet were behind him, he said, "Crew, I'm going no further until you tell me what that was. This is getting me. For a moment I almost believed in the hereafter; I thought it was here after me."

"You're not too scared," said the Bantu, chuckling. "All right. I can guess what you saw from the few words you let drop. I won't tell you what *I* saw. Then you'd really be frightened.

"Do you remember this morning when you rejected our plea and turned to walk away? What thought came to you then?"

"*Quo vadis?* Where are you going?"

"That's what we suspected," said the African, "Though in things like that we can never be sure. What we did was not so much telepathy, in the sense you think of that power. We, the four of us, summoned up our group *feeling*, the sum total of all of us, all the patterns of our bodies, focused them, and hurled that pattern of patterns to you.

"You didn't have to receive it. You could have blandly rejected it, not even knowing it was being offered you. Your 'antenna' could have been withdrawn, as it is in so many. But it wasn't. It was out, even if only a little bit. And so you picked up what we'd sent—that feeling.

"Again, I repeat, we didn't project words—that is, syllables clumped together to form individual meanings and these strung out in a false syntax. No, we gave you *us*, the concern that burned in all four. And, since it succeeded in stamping itself on you, you took it in, ferreted in your unconscious for the phrase or symbol that would most nearly match the *feeling*. Your memory came up with '*Quo vadis.*'

"See, we didn't directly speak to you. We dredged up your *response*. You, because you must explain events to yourself in terms of words, spoke to yourself in the most apt symbol. Had it been another man, one ignorant of that phrase and the story connected with it, he would have found some other thing to say to himself. You see what I mean?"

Though Crew could not see him in the dark (or could he?), Leif nodded and said, "That feeling of grief? You threw it at me?"

"Yes, though we couldn't sustain it long because you have so little experience of grief in your own being. Moreover, Mopa, the man who laughed, broke up our rapport."

"You're the machine!" the doctor broke out.

"What?"

Leif laughed and said, "I wondered where the machine was that could receive and interpret and project the semantikon: the total of all the ikons the body-mind builds, the meaning-image. I might have known it was all around me, in more senses than one. And that it had been in existence quite a few millenia."

"Your feeling gets through," said Jim Crew. His hand squeezed on Leif's. "We love you."

Leif could overlook that. That *we* made it sound impersonal. Nevertheless, he flushed with embarrassment in the dark.

He said, "If you don't explain about the horror we met a little while ago, I'm going to take this scalpel and do some fancy whittling on you."

"What his name was," said Crew, "is not known. We have a list of twelve; he could be any one of them. To tell briefly what he is, we have to go into our background. We Bantus in Africa, you know, are split up into two groups, both based originally on religious differences. Both, however, represent the only large bodies of Christendom left. The smaller nation, Chad, is dominated by the Holy Timbuktu Church, an organization that claims to have kept the teachings of our Founder uncorrupted.

"We, however, who hold central and southern Africa, believe that the Timbuktuians are an encrustation of superstition and oppressive authority."

Leif grinned to himself in the dark. The fellow was speaking out of character; his style showed that he, like many a missionary, was quoting from the book. Crew's case was only slightly different. He couldn't be accused of having read his speech, for, ten to one, he was illiterate. The Bantus frowned upon print as a device that got in the way of natural communication.

"We Primitives have, as our name indicates, resolutely stripped off *all* such bindings and returned naked to the vital Truth. We have only the very few fundamental teachings that matter; through these we have attained our present state, that is, one in which religion, mysticism, economics, politics, our whole life becomes one. We haven't allowed petty morality to stand in our way: the only code we have is the Golden Rule, which we regard as the reality . . ."

"That's enough," growled Leif. "Spare me the lecture. You're talking like a Jackass Urielite now. Reality! You know how *they* mouth that word. You should know better. In one syllable words, tell me about that man."

Crew squeezed Leif's hand again. "You're right. To be brief, we Primitives have utilized that gift once known as magic. The ancient Africans, you know, had a genius for magic. By magic I do not mean anything in a superstitious sense. Actually, magic was the misunderstood science of extra-sensory perception that those savages were using so wildly. They didn't have the control or comprehension needed to develop it.

"And when the Christianity of that day came in, plus white imperialism, the gift was weakened. But after the Apocalyptic War, there was a religious revival among the few of my people left. A great man rose among us, just as Sigmen rose among the Haijac nations. His name was Jikiza Chandu, and he was the first man to realize that we must fuse a vision of God with insight into our bodies. Fusion was his rally-cry, and . . ."

"Fuse you did," Leif concluded for him. "And what has this got to do with my question?"

For the first time since he'd known him, he detected annoyance in Crew.

The depigmented man said, "The person we just met was rejected from our society. He was a misfit, one who could not, or would not, fit into the pattern of our group. He twisted the great gifts he obtained while living as one of us and used them for evil purposes. He tried to get control over our underground here, and during his efforts he allowed so much power to flow through him that he . . . to use a simile you could understand . . . blew out a fuse. In this case, the fuse was himself.

"He, like several others who tried to become the focus of our group by force, now haunts the tunnels and sewers by day and roams the surface streets at night. They cannot hurt their own people, unless they catch us off guard, but they have done some terrible damage up there. Their victims either commit suicide or go to the insane asylums."

"Why don't you kill them? Or, at least, imprison them?"

"What? Violence on a fellow-creature?"

"You talked about reality. Isn't self-preservation real?"

"Use the sword, and you die by it. The meek shall inherit the earth. We know, because we've tested it through the centuries, that passive resistance means survival. Spill blood to save yourself for a little while, and in time you'll be drowned in the backwash."

"Indeed!"

"Pardon me, Doctor, but you saw what those

'Men In The Dark,' as we call them, can do. They use their twisted powers for the only use they can. They do not project; they reflect. That is, they can gather up the patterns of the energies broadcast by the victim, sum them up, amplify them, and send them back to the originator. He feels the abstraction, if I may call it that, absorbs it, and sees a specter that has risen from the depths of his own unconscious.

"You, if I may venture my intuition, were feeling both sad about Halla Dannto's death and guilty because you had disobeyed the CWC's orders about cremating her immediately. Also, you knew that you were going to break more commandments, that you were in love with the living Halla, and that come what might, you were going to find means to see her. Even if it meant jeopardizing the entire Plan.

"You may not even have been aware that these things were affecting you so deeply. When the 'Man in the Dark' caught what was really deepmost in you at that time, he showed it to you.

"The extraordinary thing is that the Man does not see what you do. Not at all. He senses to some extent your feeling, but he never visualizes anything. He does not know what horror he is wreaking upon you. Just the same, being insane and sadistic, he apprehends your reactions. And feeds upon them. If the victim becomes too terrified, loses his head, the Man gains more power, the force of the vision becomes more powerful, and so on.

"A Timbuktu friend of mine, versed in technical matters, explained once to me that it was an uncontrolled positive feedback. Whatever that means, the effect is terrible; J. C. save those poor souls."

"J. C. You too? What does that mean?"

"Jikiza Chandu, our Lord and Master."

"I would have thought those intials stood for your Founder."

"Oh, they do. He is Jikiza Chandu. Jikiza Chandu is He. We are all both. They are us."

No wonder, thought Leif, that the church of Timbuktu thought these fellows were the blasphemers' blasphemers.

Yet, and here he shrugged with that acceptance that so maddened his associates, they based their reasoning upon several literally taken statements, and in this they were doing no more than their bitterest opponents. Moreover, those who had been to Bantuland said that theirs was the first, and only, large human society in which one could tread almost the length and breath of a continent and find no jails, no hospitals, no insane asylums, no weapons factories (scarcely any industries, it must be admitted), no racial discrimination. And also, no lust nor love murders, no orphans, no stealing, no rich, no poor.

You could find plenty to criticize, to deplore, but your criticism didn't affect the disciples of that half-Zulu, half-Hindu prophet, Chandu.

Leif laughed, and when Jim Crew asked why, he replied, "Oh, I'm thinking about certain incredible coincidences—that when you admit there are certain unconscious rapports between minds, you see that coincidence is only a word to hide our ignorance."

"You are laughing about the J. C.'s?"

"Yes."

"Good, I laugh, too," and he did, squeezing Leif's hand again.

The doctor was about to protest when he was stopped by the Bantu.

"We're here."

Chapter 16

THE TUNNELS HAD been dark and somewhat damp and chilly. Crew opened a door, and they stepped into a country bright and hot. Nobody was there to greet them, but the Bantu insisted that his people knew the two were coming.

"Steam heat," he said in reply to the doctor's unspoken question. He calmly removed his clothes and hung them upon one of the many hooks lining the walls of the large room. Almost all the hooks were covered with garments.

"Would you care?" Jim Crew said, his hand at the hooks. Leif shook his head. The pale man said, "We thought you might want to shower."

Leif growled impatiently at the man who had stepped into the shower. "I thought we were in such a hurry to look at your child."

The Bantu stepped out and still naked and dripping walked into another room. "Follow us, doctor. That shower took only a minute. And it was much more than you could see—it was a ceremony, one we Primitives always perform when we return home. It was also a prayer, a combination of physical and psychic cleansing and an asking of J. C. that Anadi might be served. At the same time, we communicated with those who are holding hands and found out that Anadi will endure until you get to her.''

He led the surgeon through several small rooms, some of which had bunks lining the walls. One had an altar with a man hanging from a crucifix. His skin was black, and the face was an abstraction, belonging to no race except that which has suffered but has felt the touch of a hand that smooths out all lines of pain. If Leif had had more time, he would have stopped to discuss the sculptor and his technique with Crew. He had heard that the Bantus were the great artists of today, that they were doing things nobody had ever done before in painting, sculpture and music.

The first men and women they met were unclothed, like Crew. They crowded around the newcomer and swarmed over him, kissing and fondling him. He returned their caresses and then made swift introductions. One of the girls was a steatopygous Diana whose imperfect depigmentation had left her freckled with huge spots. She clung to Leif's neck and whispered that she loved him.

"Brindled Beatrice, I love you, too," he replied and dismissed her with a slap.

"Someday you should examine that levity and see what it is hiding," remarked Crew.

Despite Leif's joking, the sweat had popped out on his head in a profusion even the steam heat couldn't account for. He was beginning to wonder what he'd let himself in for. His simple errand of mercy was far from simple.

Jim Crew took his hand and led him through another series of rooms. As the walls were concrete and painted over with murals, many of which were peeling already, Leif could not tell what these

chambers had once been used for. In some the floors
and sides had split wide open to admit earth, oozing
through like blood in a wound, or to show hard rock
behind.

Every place held a half dozen or so people who
greeted Jim demonstratively and then rose to follow
the two. Once Leif looked over his shoulder. They
had formed a long line, two abreast, male and
female, each pair holding hands and placing their
outside hands on the shoulders of the person ahead
of them. The sexes were staggered, so that each man
had his outstretched fingers upon the skin of a
woman in front, and the woman in her turn touched
the back of a man.

A low mutter arose; man and woman chanting a
whispering phone and antiphone. Though he could
not make out the individual words, which he was sure
were in Swahili, he felt the hairs rise on his neck. It
sounded and *felt* like a thunderstorm gathering in the
hills, ready to break, stretching the air with lightning-
streaks in embryo.

He was glad when they finally stopped in the room
where the little girl lay. Unconscious, she was
stretched out upon a bed. A man and a woman
crouched by her, her hands in theirs. Beside them
stood a tall Negro, clothed in black and wearing a
white collar turned backwards. He looked up at Leif
through thick lenses and horn-rimmed glasses.

"Ah, Doctor Barker," he said, stepping up and
holding his hand out. Leif shook it while Crew said
that this was the Reverend Anthony Djouba. A mem-
ber of the Timbuktu underground, he was also a doctor. Crew's friends had not hesitated in contacting
him for aid for Anadi. Apparently, the two sects did
work together now and then.

Leif examined the framework of wire and sponge
rubber and quickdrying plaster that held the girl's
skull together.

"Very good," he said. "You did this, *abba*?"

Djouba replied in a high, thin voice, "Yes, I brought along all the materials I had. They're not much, but they'll help."

Leif examined his bag and agreed with him. Then he looked into the top of the cast around Anadi's head, whistling as he did so at what he saw. She should have died instantly. That she hadn't and that she still lived was to him proof that she possessed something extraordinary. For the first time, he began to wonder if, actually, there was more than a sort of modified black magic to this talk about "holding hands."

Djouba, looking over his shoulder, "tsk-tsked" and said, "Pieces of bone in her brain. Even if we save her, doctor, I'm afraid she'll be an idiot."

Impersonally, the two discussed what they would do, then laid out their tools. Leif began to sterilize his equipment. Crew insisted that it wasn't necessary. None of them feared germs; their bodies could handle the most virulent. Leif silenced him. He was the doctor; he was doing this operation. Get busy and scrub down the table. As soon as that was done, he and his friend should put Anadi on it.

Lifting Anadi was easy, as she weighed no more than ninety pounds. Immediately afterwards, Leif began working. For six hours he bent over the incredibly shattered cranium and injured brain. Then, exhausted, hands on the verge of trembling, he extracted the last fragment of bone and deposited upon the gray mass a thick film of blue-print jelly. Djouba then capped the open skull with a plastic arch. At this point Crew protested again that the artificial top would not be needed. Anadi, he maintained, would in time regrow her own skull.

"In that case," replied Leif, making no attempt to hide his incredulity, "you may remove the cap whenever you want to. But I'd like to see that when it happens."

Djouba removed his thick glasses and polished them.

"Much as I hate to give these people credit for anything," he said, "I'll have to admit that she may do just that. I saw some strange things while I was a missionary in Bantuland."

"But bone, doctor! I can barely conceive that a human being might, through advanced self-awareness, rediscover the lost faculty of regeneration of flesh. But bone!"

Djouba put his glasses back on. His eyes grew enormous behind the lenses.

"I didn't say she could. I said she might." Djouba smiled at Leif.

"I'd like to get going," said Leif, impatiently, not wishing to become too involved with these people.

"Wouldn't you two like to eat first?" asked one of the women. She was the Brindled Beatrice.

"I would," he said.

Djouba hesitated.

Crew said, "It is about the only way we can now pay you, *abba*. As for the future, who knows?"

"Anadi does," shrilled the Brindled Beatrice. "She always could tell the future."

"I'll stay," said Djouba. Then smiling, "If she could look ahead into time, why didn't she avoid getting her skull crushed?"

"She must have had a good reason. She'll tell us when she mends. As for now, let's eat."

They went into a very large room that Leif suspected had once been a waiting room for an ancient subway. There they sat down to hot locust soup, freshly baked bread, candied yams, bananas and milk. Brindled Beatrice, who insisted upon sitting next to Leif, said that some of the food had been

stolen or else contributed by Jack converts, but
that most of it was shipped in through a secret
method.

From the hints she dropped, he got the impression
the food came by underwater, perhaps in a spaceship
that crept under the surface of the Seine to Paris and
discharged its cargo through a submerged lock. This
surprised him, for he thought the Bantus had no
complicated craft.

While they talked, the people in the background
chanted softly. When the meal was over, and thanks
had been given, all the Bantus sang the low hint-of-
thunder song that had raised his hackles when he was
being led to Anadi. As some cleared away the dishes,
the others formed into the same pairings of male and
female. This time, they made six concentric circles.
Each circle was linked to the next by a man and
woman who kept their backs to each other and their
palms against the breasts or back of a person in the
human rings.

Djouba, on Leif's other side, shifted uneasily sand
said, "They might at least have considered me and
waited until I was gone. After all I did for them,
too."

He put his spoon down and rose.

Leif said, "What's the matter?"

He started to rise but was pulled back by his
freckled companion.

"Lover, let him go," she crooned.

"Have some respect for my cloth!" shouted
Djouba.

"We love you!" came the response.

"I don't want that kind of love!"

"We love you!" crashed the surf.

"God forgive you for that blasphemy!"

Unhearing, the circles began to sway back and
forth, to rotate in little hops and shuffles.

Jim Crew sprang upon the table that was the center of the six rims. Flinging up his arms, he yelled, "Who's our lover?"

The throats became one vast megaphone, bellowing in Leif's ears.

"Jikiza Chandu!"

"And whom do we love?"

"Jikiza Chandu!"

"And who are we?"

"Jikiza Chandu!"

"And who is he?"

"Jikiza Chandu!"

"And who loves Dr. Djouba?"

"Jikiza Chandu!"

"No, no!" screamed the Timbuktuian. "Stop this outrage! Let me out!"

"And who loves Dr. Barker?"

"Jikiza Chandu!"

"And who is Djouba?"

"Jikiza Chandu!"

"And who is Dr. Barker?"

"Jikiza Chandu!"

"And who is the lover and the beloved, the god and the man, the creator and the created, the man and the woman?"

"Jikiza Chandu!"

"And what does Jikiza Chandu say?"

Now the circles were whirling faster, faster, the people who formed them kept from whirling away by linking hands together. Their faces were contorted. Their mouths were wide, lips drawn back. Their eyes were glowing blue ovals. Their nostrils flared and snorted. Teeth shone wetly; spittle flew.

There was a sudden stoppage of the shouts that had echoed and re-echoed from the far-off walls; there was only the stomp and slap of bare feet and the sound of their harsh breathing. Torsos shook so that flesh rippled like groundwaves. Hips rotated or stabbed so violently they looked as if they must dislocate pelvises.

Then, following the audible sucking in of breath, the visible swelling of chests, a mighty word was hurled against the walls and against the ears of all doubters.

"Love!"

"Love." screamed the Brindled Beatrice.

Where he might in a difference place and under different circumstances have enjoyed this ardent female, he now had but one idea, and that was the same as Djouba's—*get out!*

In about sixty seconds, he'd scrambled, jumped, pushed, crawled and run through the flailing bodies, waving arms and clutching hands. Once he reached haven, he turned and saw that the Chadian was close behind him. His tattered clothes, rent from him by the crowd, were held to his chest in clutching hands.

"God help me!" Djouba panted. "That is a new type of martyrdom!"

Leif had regained some of his detachment.

"You're a saint now?"

The Chadian adjusted his glasses. Recovered sight seemed to add to his assurance.

"Only a matter of speaking."

He looked at the room.

"Unspeakable!"

"They're just expressing their love. And you must admit that not only are they not hypocrites, but they seem to have affection enough for everybody."

"Gross carnality!"

Djouba shuddered and glanced down at his body.

"We can get clothes for you in the entrance," said Leif, not unkindly. "They're rags, but they'll keep the bold eyes and the chill off."

"I can't understand why they did this to me. After all, I kept their child from dying until you arrived."

"A matter of viewpoint. The whole affair was a thanksgiving because we helped to save her."

"I note you were just as eager as I to leave."

Leif shrugged and said, "I've been raised in a different culture from yours, but like yourself I failed to adjust to theirs. They must have something. Besides their development of psychosomatic powers, they've the most nearly perfect society on Earth. Compare theirs with yours, doctor . . . you deride their religion and deplore their social customs, yet you'll have to admit that your native land of Chad has many criminals, murderers, poor and crippled. And theirs has almost none."

Djouba began searching on the racks for the cleanest clothes he could find. Stiffy, he replied, "That has nothing to do with it. You saw what went on in that room. Do you think the Founder of our church, the One they also claim is theirs, would approve?"

"I don't know. Who does? Weigh his country and yours in the balance, who sinks, who rises? I say, judge an action by its effect upon people. What they're doing is hurting nobody in their society. The same behavior in our lands would cause harm."

"I can see there's no use discussing this with you. There is an absolute, you know."

"No, I don't. Absolute what?"

The answer was an absolute silence that hung heavy until Jim Crew appeared. Contrary to what they expected, he did not look hangdog or exhausted. His step was brisk; his face, beaming.

"Ah, doctors, we hope you enjoyed yourselves. And if ever we can help you, call on us. Love knows no bounds; we must help our fellows. Your escort, Dr. Djouba, will be here in just a minute. And we'll take you back to the surface, Dr. Barker, by another route. Through the basement of a purification palace reserved for the hierarchy, 'The Abode of the Blessed.' "

Chapter 17

IT WAS CLOSE to dawn when Leif walked into the Rigorous Mercy Hospital. The sleepy Uzzite on duty at the personnel door scanned the lamech with his flash and then told the doctor to pass.

Dwelling on the lack of precautions, Leif stepped into the elevator, and shot up to the penthouse. When he walked into the hall, he did not find, as he had expected, another guard before his door. After unlocking the door, he discovered why.

The house was empty; Halla and Ava were gone.

He didn't waste time but at once QB'd Rachel. Hair in curlers, wrapped in a frayed white gown, she answered. When she saw him, her eyes threw out sleep and widened into wakefulness.

"All right, Rachel!" he snapped. "Tell me quick what happened."

He did not add that he wanted the information before Candleman could get to him. It was more than probable that an Uzzite was listening in on him at that moment.

Rachel gasped that she'd thought he'd been kidnapped; how in the name of Sigmen had he escaped? When he told her never mind, just give him the developments, she replied crossly that she didn't know what he wanted to know. He tore his hair and shouted that if she didn't tell him quick where Mrs. Dannto and Ava were, he would climb through the QB and tear her limb from limb.

Rachel replied that they were in Montreal. After Leif had supposedly been kidnaped by Jacques Cuze, Candleman had insisted that Dannto and his wife take the Canadian rocket. He'd also wanted Ava to go along as the woman's nurse. All three, he swore, were in danger. And though Ava had refused at first, she'd given in.

Leif thought that Ava must have had strong reasons for doing so. Something must have come up that necessitated her remaining with Halla.

At his request, Rachel left her little room and went into the office. She came back with a book that listed that day's business. After she'd read the records of the QB calls and the mail, he gleaned one item that interested him. That stupid Z. Roe, as Rachel termed him, had QB'd to find out if he should appear for another eegie in the morning. And she'd denied him twice before.

So Zack was looking for him, eh? Probably with orders for everything from a complete report of what had happened to a request for his appearance at a drumhead court-martial. Leif had long suspected that this grey-headed old man was anything but the cipher he seemed, that he was, actually, Leif's superior. Though the doctor had always thought of himself as the leader of the Parisian CWC, he had had evidence from time to time that his decisions were being countermanded and that someone was checking up on him. It had been, in a way, laughable that the Marchers should have absorbed so much of the suspicion of the very people they were fighting.

Now, Leif saw little humor in the situation.

"Any messages from Ava?" he asked.

"None, Doctor Barker."

He looked at Rachel's unrouged pale face and the curlers and wondered what he'd ever seen enticing in her. "Go back to bed, girl," he said gently. "I'll see you in the morning."

When her image faded, he made himself some coffee and over the searing black liquid decided to contact Zack Roe as soon as possible. Before he'd drained the cup, he heard somebody unlocking his door. It couldn't be Ava, so he was prepared when Candleman walked in.

The Uzzite's face was as ever, the long, narrow skull and sweeping jaw forming a bedrock for the rigid flesh above. The thin figure moved a trifle jerkily, reminding Leif of a marionette. Candleman, he imagined, was both master and puppet, part of him poised above himself, carefully controlling the part on the stage, yet never able to conceal the strings nor move the limbs with lifelike smoothness.

Leif, prepared for anything except what happened, was surprised when Candleman calmly monotoned a request for Barker's experiences with Jacques Cuze.

That put Leif on a tightrope. He could cover up the existence of Jim Crew's comrades with a lie. On the other hand, Candleman might know more than he seemed to; he might be baiting him.

Leif decided on his story almost as soon as the Uzzite had quit talking and had leaned forward, sharp nose eager, parrot-like beak lips pressed, and grey eyes crouched.

"You are correct, Candleman," he said, and gave him what he wanted to hear.

The Uzzite stood up. His eyes, usually lusterless as a mouse's fur, shone, and his voice rose.

"So this fellow that forced you at gunpoint to operate on his daughter called himself Jim Crew?

Can't you see what I see? No? Think, Doctor, think! The initials!''

Leif struck the table with his fist. Coffee sloshed over the plastic top.

"Time's end!" he swore. "So they are!"

"Absolutely. You say these fellows were foreign-looking and they spoke in a tongue neither Haijac nor Hebrew. It must have been French! Sigmen, I wish I knew something of that language!"

I hope you never take the trouble to study it, thought the doctor.

Candleman began pacing back and forth. Lightly, he flicked the seven-thonged whip back and forth.

"Doctor, my natural inclination would be to call together all my available men and conduct a manhunt on a scale never before done. But I'm not going to. Jacques Cuze is a cunning fox; he'll be hiding low for quite a while. And I've no doubt he's moved from the place you describe.''

At that moment the QB glowed, and the operator's voice said, "Montreal calling, Dr. Barker.''

Leif acknowledged and saw the cube become a room in which sat the Sandalphon, Halla and Ava. Dannto said, "Barker! Candleman called and told us you were back. Sigmen be praised! No, don't explain now. You two jump into a special and come here at once. I've authorized a rocket to be set aside for you. Your assistant will take over your duties. I want you to look Halla over. She complains of pains in her solar plexus. Also, we can hear your story face to face, and later we can go to Metatron Wong's big estate in the forest for a little relaxation. That's all. May your future be real.''

The cube flickered into transparency.

Leif rose to protest, for he wanted to find out about Halla and Ava. Also his heart was tight with longing for the redhaired woman.

Candleman arose and said, "Since his wife's back, Dannto's his old self."

"Since she's back?"

"Yes, they were separated just before her 'accident.' She, I presume, wanted something, and he wouldn't let her have it. So she moved to another apartment. It's happened before. And always the Sandalphon gives in." The Uzzite snorted. "I can remember when no woman would have dared. She'd either have been whipped or sent to H. But this woman has made him lose his senses."

"You're criticising the Sturch-head?" Leif asked gently.

"You've no record of my words," said Candleman. "Anyway, Dannto knows how I feel about this woman's influence on him."

He said nothing further while Leif packed. Presently, the two of them walked onto the roof of the hospital and waited for the special. When it sank beside them, they entered and sat down side by side. During the entire trip, Candleman was silent. Once he sat up, looking at Leif, and said, "Dr. Barker, you seem to be a very happy, free and easy fellow. Is it because you have a fine wife?"

Then, before the astonished doctor could reply, the Uzzite said, "I withdraw that. Please forgive me. I've no business asking." And he muttered, "Not in the line of duty, you know."

Barker wondered what was going on behind that blond Dante's face. He wished he could have put the 'picker on him.

That wish led to another, which was his desire to know whether or not Trausti and Palsson had been questioned. If they had, they must have certified Candleman's suspicions about Leif's behavior. Possibly Candleman was taking him away from Paris so that he might not be able to deal with the two informers. And he might have put Dannto up to inviting Leif to Montreal so he could watch him when he was with Ava and Halla.

He dwelt upon the redheaded beauty and just what she might be. He pondered her origins and during his speculations found himself abandoning all except one thought: he was fascinated by her as he'd never been by any other woman, and he had to be with her.

Much as he resented this irresistible attraction, he had to go to her. Perhaps the moth resented his passion for the flame; yet the moth flew headlong into it.

Shortly before they landed at the airport, one of Candleman's lieutenants got permission from the two lamechians to switch on the QB for a news report. The gandyman sprang into view in the middle of a sentence. He was describing a recent riot in Chicago in which a man had been torn apart by an infuriated crowd. It seemed the culprit had said that he didn't think Timestop was at all near. According to Sigmen, so he claimed, conditions in the Haijac would be perfect before he arrived from his timevoyagings. This man didn't think that the setup was near perfection.

"Immediately thereafter," honked the gandyman. "an enraged mob avenged this insult to the Union, to the Sturch and to Sigmen, real be his name. And now, good citizens, we take you . . ." and the scene in the cube dissolved. When it resolved, it showed a street empty except for a few Uzzites. They surrounded a pool of blood and a leg lying on a curb.

Leif looked at it keenly before the vision blurred. When he sat back, he smiled. His professional eye had noticed at once that the limb had not been torn, but had been expertly severed. Undoubtedly, this was some of the Sturch's propaganda-pressuring. Faked.

He doubted that any crowd in the Haijac would be

able to whip up enough enthusiasm or organization to lynch a man. The ordinary citizen was too busy working night and day to clothe and feed himself and too scared of going to H to make a move without his gapt's approval.

To keep from falling asleep, Leif asked Candleman what Mrs. Dannto had told him about her accident. Candleman said, "Her story is about what I guessed it to be."

He paused to smack his hardshelled lips and continued, "All she knows is that she received a call over the commie. She didn't recognize the voice, and the man speaking said the QB on his end wasn't working. She believed him because that frequently happens. He said his name was Jarl Covers—" the Uzzite glanced significantly at Leif—"and that he was a lieutenant of mine. That, of course, was a lie. Mrs. Dannto should have checked to see if there was a Covers on my force.

"He said that he wanted to meet her to discuss a plot against her husband's life. Covers claimed he'd stumbled across it but couldn't go to his superiors about it because some of them were the instigators. I suppose the fellow was trying to throw suspicion on me. Since Dannto himself was in Montreal, Covers wanted to talk to Dannto's wife. She was terrified and unable to think straight. She went out in a taxi to meet Covers. The man I'd detailed to guard her while her husband was gone was answering another call, presumably from Covers' accomplice. That was his story; he's being questioned very closely about it.

"That is all we know."

Leif had wondered what story Halla would give. It was a good one, for it aroused Candleman's suspicions about Jacques Cuze and threw a hot haze before his otherwise cold and clear thinking. Nor could the story be checked on, because calls to the

Sandalphon's house were not monitored.

There remained one mystery. Who *had* called the original Halla to her death?

Wondering, he fell asleep. Once, he awoke when the ship landed. Candleman said they'd just received word to go on to the Metatron's estate in the big woods. Leif drifted back and did not come out of his doze until the door opened. Yawning, blinking, he walked into the hot Canadian noonshine. A runabout picked them up and flew them in a minute to the summer mansion of the political head of North America.

It was quite a party that the men walked into. Most of the important men of the Haijac were gathered upon the front lawn. Their wives and mistresses were with them; all were in hunting costume. Leif was met by Dannto and Halla and introduced to everybody. His reputation as a brain surgeon was widespread, and most of them knew of him.

Then he was given hunting clothes and rifle and ammo. While he dressed behind a screen, he gave to the Sandalphon and others who could crowd into the room the same story he'd told Candleman. At its end, Dannto said, "You were lucky they didn't kill you afterwards."

He turned to Candleman and said, "I suppose you still insist this Jim Crew is Jacques Cuze? How ridiculous can you get? Anybody who wasn't a monomaniac could see his initials stand for Jude Changer."

There was a murmur of agreement, for the majority were Urielites. Candleman did not turn expression, but Leif got the feeling of resentment on his part.

Leif examined the man.

Not too long ago, he thought, the governors of the Haijac were men built like Candleman, tall, bony, with long narrow faces and dour lips. They burned day and night with zeal for the Sturch, nor at any time could you have caught them in an unreal act.

Now they had been replaced with men like Dannto, the shorter, much stouter and more garrulous executive. Though they discussed abstract principles, they were more likely to be found dealing with the immediate and the knowable. And, as now, you could smell the aroma of very good liquor, and you could see they had chosen their women, not for the oldfashioned virtues of frigidity and fertility and faithfulness to the Sturch, but for their red lips and full figures and devotion to their men.

Leif went back out onto the lawn. There he got a chance to talk for a moment with Ava and Halla. The only one near was the Uzzite, and he was out of ear-shot.

"Did Zack Roe or anybody else say anything about my having gone underground with Crew?" asked Leif.

Ava smiled strangely. "No. Nobody knew where you were."

"I couldn't contact you over the QB. You know that."

"Leif, I wouldn't be in your shoes. And all because of her."

Ava gestured at the woman.

Halla said, "You needn't look so contemptuous."

"What's this?" asked Leif.

"I wondered about her," replied Ava, "so, while you were gone and she was still sleeping, I examined her. That was enough to lead me to making X-rays of her. When she awoke, I made her tell me what she was."

"So I did," said Halla, speaking very low but very fast. "And Ava recoiled as if I were a poisonous spider. She acted as though she hated me and would like to see me dead. It was then she told me my sister was dead."

"Why did you do that?" demanded Leif. He felt his face getting hot and his hands cold.

Ava shifted uneasily, but finally looked him straight in the eye.

"I wanted to discharge her grief then. If she found out by accident about the real Halla, she might be overcome at a time when there'd be no explaining it. I gave her a grief-runner. She had no deeprooted anxieties holding her sorrow in, so she got rid of it in about half an hour. Now there's nothing to worry about."

"You lie in your teeth," snapped the redhead. "You loathe me because of what I have been doing. Yet it's been for our country. You told me about my sister so you could hurt me. I won't forget that."

"Watch it," said Leif. "Candleman's coming."

He whispered to Ava, "First chance you get, tell me all about it." Ava nodded and glanced at Halla and said, "You won't even want to touch her when I explain, Leif. Or maybe you will, being what you are."

Halla turned away suddenly, but not before Leif saw the tears . . .

His chance to talk to Ava came after they'd been transported some hundred miles to the hunting lodge.

Chapter 18

BEFORE SETTING OUT for the hunting, the party was briefed by Lwi Rulo, the chief guide. He told them that their quarry would be Neanderthaloids imported from the third planet of the star Gemma. The Neanderthaloids were the dominant life form of Gemma III, and were potentially as intelligent as Terrestrials. But at the time the first spaceship from the Haijac Union landed, the Gemmans were in a stage of culture roughly corresponding to the Bronze Age of Earth. That is, the highest culture of Gemma was at that point. But a great part of the planet was in the Old and/or New Stone Age, and the Gemmans imported for the hunt were of the Neolithic stage. Unarmed, they had been released several hours ago. But flint and chert were available in this region, and the Gemmans could in a very short time chip our spear and arrow heads and arm themselves. Thus, though equipped with inferior weapons, they were dangerous game, not to be treated with contempt.

"Only last year two of our hunting party were killed and one wounded," said Lwi Rulo. "The

Urielite Gundarsson was pierced with an arrow. The Uzzite Smith was disemboweled with a spear, and his wife was wounded in the shoulder.''

Leif smiled. The Urielite Gundarsson had been killed by a March CWC-man disguised as a Gemman. The Marcher had shot the Jack with a wooden-shafted flint-tipped arrow, but the bow was of laminated maple and fiberglass. The Marcher was standing in the bushes a hundred yards off when he had sent the arrow crashing through the man's chest. Then the bowman had faded away into the Canadian woods and been picked up by a plane. Later, a Marcher in the hierarchy had stepped up into the shoes of the dead man, where he was in a better position to do more damage to the Haijac Union.

Lwi Rulo ended his instruction by warning the group that they must not string out but must stay close together. There would be no beaters going ahead of them to flush the game.

The party set out, laughing, chattering as if they were going to hunt rabbits. The hot summer sun burned down, the trees were tall and green, birds sang, everything seemed all right in the world. In a short time they had forgotten Rulo's words and had separated into small groups and couples that gradually drifted away from each other.

Leif had been waiting for this to happen. He gestured Ava to one side.

"All right!" he said fiercely. "Tell me what you found out from Halla?"

"Halla—or, rather, Erica, for that is her real name—is one of us—though I hate to say it. She belongs to the CWC. So did her twin sister. They were part of a group trained to do their work among the hierarchy. And very successfully, too, though I despise them for what they're doing. War is a dirty business, Leif, but I didn't think it would become this dirty! Or that we'd be the ones who'd stoop so low!"

"Doing what?" said Leif. "Why're you so bitter? Is Halla an extraterrestrial? What's wrong with using them if they can help us? Come on, tell me."

"No, they're not XT's," said Ava through clenched teeth. "I wish they weren't human! Then there'd be some excuse for their doing their filthy work!"

"They're not XT's then? Then why those alien organs? I don't understand."

"Apparently biological science in our country is even more advanced that we thought. You've been among the Jacks too long to keep up with the latest developments in March. Though I doubt if even you would have heard of this, for it must be a super hush-hush project."

"Are you saying that these organs were developed in our laboratories and that they were surgically implanted in Halla and the other women?"

"Shib."

"But what are those organs for?"

"Walk slower." said Ava. "We're catching up with the Danntos."

Leif slowed the pace. He looked ahead, where Dannto and Halla and several other Urielites and their women were. These had halted while a guide searched the thick brush to make sure no Gemmans were hiding there.

Ava spoke softly, "I can't explain everything in one or two sentences. But I will try to be brief. Though I may not seem to you to be getting to the point as fast as I should.

"You know that one of the bases of Haijac culture is the repression of sexual instincts, the deliberate training of children, and hence the adults, to regard sex as a necessary evil. There must be no joy in the act, even when it's done with one's spouse. Of course, I agree with the Jacks up to a point. It is an evil act if it's done outside the bounds of matrimony. But it is holy between man and wife . . ."

"I know your beliefs. Tell me about these women."

"First, I have to tell you why these women exist. The Jack theory is that very sexually repressed people are more subservient and hence amenable to totalitarian government. They are, in effect, castrated. And they have a personality which the Sturch desires. Narrow-minded. Upright. Dedicated to the Sturch. Suspicious. Ready to betray any suspected deviationist to the Sturch. Unfortunately for the people involved, one of the results of such repression is frigidity, impotency.

"By impotency I don't mean so much an incapability to perform the sexual act as an inability to have a complete or satisfactory orgasm. Orgasm is a thing to be ashamed of. In fact, as you know, the Sturch approves of artificial insemination. But powerful as the Sturch is, it hasn't dared to make artificial insemination a law. It has had to recommend it and to arrange that only those who practice it gain success in the Union. Theoretically, you can't be a lamech-wearer unless you renounce the sex act. But . . ."

"Get to the point!" snapped Leif.

"Shib. I'm trying. If the sexual drive is distorted, it must have an outlet somewhere. And it does. Sex is sublimated into fanaticism and hate. Hence the willingness of the Jack to betray his fellows. Hence the government-sponsored pogroms of the so-called unrealists."

"Wait a minute!" said Leif. He had been watching a clump of heavily-leaved bushes, some of whose branches were moving in a suspicious manner. Determined though he was to hear Ava out, he did not want Halla to be jumped by a Gemman.

A guide stopped the party again while he explored the bushes. After a few minutes he waved to the hunters to come head.

"Candleman is watching us," said Leif. "He'll be over here before long, and we'll have no chance to talk."

"Some evil genius in the Cold War Corps," said Ava, "conceived an idea to take advantage of the frigidity of the Haijac male. Some biological genius. He created that organ you found in the dead woman. You know we've been able to create low forms of life. This organ wasn't as difficult to grow in the laboratory as the layman might think. Especially since it was designed for a simple purpose."

Ava stopped, for somewhere to their right was a commotion. The wind brought shouts and a scream. Then, the rapid firing of rifles.

"They found one of the poor devils," said Leif. "I hope he made them pay dearly."

"Candleman is edging this way," said Ava. "I'd better get this over with."

Ava continued in a very low voice, "This organism was designed to be a bio-electrical battery. It released a flow of electrical current during excitation of the woman in whom it was implanted."

"Ah, I see!" said Leif. "And caused the male to have a complete orgasm. The current flowed from the highly charged body—the woman's—to the less highly charged body—the man's! And the current was strong enough to break down the conditioned reflexes which caused the frigidity of the male. Willynilly, he had, for the first time in his life, a complete and natural reaction to sexual intercourse! And, of course . . ."

"Of course, he wasn't going to allow the woman

responsible to get away from him. The woman would have great influence over him. And the woman, of course, was a March agent.''

"What a brilliant idea!" said Leif.

"It's just like you to admire it," said Ava bitterly. "I think it's evil and abhorrent."

For one of the few times in his life, Leif was flabbergasted.

"You're objecting on moral grounds? Why? This is war! You don't object to killing in war. God knows you've murdered enough Jacks in the past ten years!"

"Killing for your country is one thing," said Ava. "But this—this use of fornication as a weapon—it's unspeakable!"

Leif threw his hands up in a gesture of despair and disgust.

"I give up!"

He paused and frowned as if he were thinking deeply. Then he reddened and said, "Something just occurred to me. The CWC may not have thought of it. Is Halla a virgin? If she is, how is she going to explain her virginity to Dannto?"

Ava veiled big black eyes and said, "I took care of that."

Leif grabbed the slender arm and squeezed so hard Ava cried with pain and dropped the rifle.

"You . . . you!" Leif choked. "How?"

"Surgically, of course. What did you think?"

"You know what I'm thinking."

"What's the matter, Leif? Were you planning—"

"Quiet. Here comes Candleman."

Ava stopped and picked up the rifle. The Uzzite, carrying his in the crook of his arm, walked up to them with his habitual crouch. He opened his mouth to say something, when he was interrupted by a scream.

All three whirled. The voice had been Halla

Dannto's; now, she was speechless. Paralyzed, she held her throat with one hand and pointed with the other.

Leif took one look at the brutish, skinclad figure charging at her with a spear and brought his rifle up. Until then he'd had no intention if shooting down the Gemmans imported for the sport of Neros. He'd hoped that some of the Neanderthaloids might maim or kill some of their Jack hunters; it would serve them right.

Now, he didn't hesitate, but in one fluid motion brought the barrel up, aiming it a trifle ahead of the gorilla chest, and squeezed the trigger. His was a .45 recoilless; he scarcely felt the jar; before he could place another shot, he heard Candleman's blast, only a trifle later than his, and he saw the Gemman fall sideways.

Dannto had stepped in front of Halla. Now, seeing the apeman jerking on the ground, he stood there, pale and quivering. Candleman, however, ran up and placed his muzzle against the upturned face and blew it apart with dumdum after dumdum.

Leif could see that Halla was unhurt. He didn't waste time asking her if she were all right, as Dannto was doing. Instead, he bent over the corpse.

Ava, following, said, "Where did he get those leather things to bind the spear head to the shaft? And, if you'll notice, the shaft is of seasoned wood."

Candleman came back in time to hear the last of these remarks.

"One of the Sandalphon's enemies undoubtedly did that," he said. "I'll order an immediate investigation of the servants who handle these Gemmans."

The Danntos walked up and looked at the corpse. Halla was white. Her lips were scarlet spatters.

Leif looked at the others. None of them seemed to see what he had seen. He decided to keep silent.

However, to satisfy completely his curiosity, he knelt down and examined the body more carefully. He lifted the animal skin wrapped around the torso, saw something he'd not expected, and dropped it. When he rose, his lips were tightly pressed, as if he were having trouble containing himself.

Ava, sensitive to his actions, saw he was concerned, but she said nothing until they were again a little separate from the others.

"What did you see, Leif?"

He said, "Didn't you observe the proportions of the corpse's legs and arms? A Gemman's arms, compared to a man's, are short, as are the legs. The bones of the forearms are bowed out to serve as attachments for the mighty muscles. The neck-vertebrae are curved so that the Gemman, like the ape, can't bend his neck back to look upwards. There are other differences, but I won't go into detail.

"That fellow had longer arms and legs than he should have had. His radius and ulna were straight as a man's. His neck, though so thick it almost didn't exist, was quite capable of bending back. In short, he was a man. I'll bet that if his face hadn't been destroyed, we'd have seen that pseudoskin had been built up on it to make it look Neanderthal.

"But that wasn't all. Somebody wanted to disguise his real purpose. A small J.C. had been tattooed on his belly."

Ava took it calmly.

"Obviously, if he were killed, Cuze or Changer would get the blame. But what if he'd not been?"

"Five gets you one he had the usual poison tooth. You'll notice he made for Halla. Does that tie in with the 'accident' her sister was in?"

"What do you think? The question is, why these attempts on her life? Why is Jacques Cuze being blamed?"

"Tune in on the next chapter and find out," said Leif.

"Be serious! Why didn't you tell the rest of them what you found out?"

"Listen, whoever put that man up to an assassination attempt on Halla must have been nearby. He wanted to be able to kill the man so that if he were caught, he could stop his mouth. Perhaps he planned on doing it anway. Corpses don't talk. Whoever wanted Halla murdered was premeditatedly close."

"That would include only two dozen people. What about Candleman? He ran up and destroyed the man's face. It looks to me as if he was trying to hide the fellow's identity."

"Candleman shot almost the same time I did. If he were behind the affair, he would have waited until the spear was in Halla. And butchering the face wouldn't conceal anything. There's always the fingerprints. I'm planning on getting those later and doing some checking up from there. Besides—getting back to Candleman—though he doesn't like Halla, he is very devoted to Dannto."

"Leif, the man who killed the first Halla was in Paris. This is Canada. He'd have to come here when we did. Who came with Dannto? Who came with you?"

"There are at least twenty big brass who came from Europe at the Metatron's invitation. Do you want me to question them all?"

"All we can do is wait for another attempt."

"That ought to make you happy. You hate Halla, anyway."

"Yes, but she's CWC."

"Don't forget that," said Leif. "You hang around and get those fingerprints, if you can. As for me, I've work to do."

Boldly, he walked up to where Halla sat upon a stump and Dannto stood by, holding her hand.

"Mrs. Dannto has had a shock," said Leif. "She shouldn't continue the hunt. I'm not really interested in this shooting, and since I'm her doctor, I'll take her back to the Metatron's. Would you care to come along, Sandalphon? If not, you really won't be needed."

Dannto obviously wanted to be with his wife. The doctor, however, had loudly stated before a dozen high officials that he didn't have to go with her. That was malice aforethought; Leif knew that the Urielite would consider it a matter of face to continue the hunt. He would be afraid the others might think he'd been too unnerved by the surprise attack.

So, as Barker had guessed he would, Dannto bellowed that he, personally, wanted to kill every Gemman now hiding in the Canadian woods. The others standing round nodded their heads and slapped him on the shoulder and said by Sigmen they'd be glad to give him first shot.

Nevertheless, the Archurielite's mouth formed a pout of disappointment when he saw Leif hand his wife into a Hill runabout.

He waddled clumsily over at the last moment and kissed her pale cheek and said he'd bring her one or two heads.

Halla shuddered and didn't reply.

"Take good care of her, doctor," said Dannto as the Hill rose into the air.

Leif's reply didn't seem to erase the lines from Dannto's forehead.

"*Abba*, she'll get taken care of as never before."

Chapter 19

HE CONDUCTED HER to the Sandalphon's suite and dismissed the maid who was cleaning it. Though she was undoubtedly bound to report it to the Uzzites, he did not care. His lamech and his surgeon's license gave him more freedom than the average Jack.

Halla closed the door and inserted in the lock a frequency-key.

"My aunts will QB Dannto that I'm all right," she said.

Her every movement and word stroked soft and warm fingers over his skin. Suddenly, his breath caught, and he felt a tightening within his chest. His hands and the back of his neck trembled.

She turned from the door and walked across the room towards a bureau. Whether consciously or unconsciously, her hips swayed just a trifle more than they normally did. Leif knew, for he'd watched her often enough that day. There was no doubt about it. From the moment she had glanced at him to say she wanted to be alone, the air had become charged. If the sudden feeling grew more intense, he would, he was sure, explode. He was fighting an internal pressure; something was building up in him; it had been there for a long time, latent, waiting to be started by the glance, the movement.

"Halla!" he said, low and husky, almost unable to speak.

She stopped, her back turned partly to him, her spine stiffening, the abrupt rigidity raising the full breasts. A small toss of the head sent light rippling down the long red hair.

"Halla, do I have to say anything?"

She whirled so fast she almost lost her balance. It was a movement that would at another time have made him grin. Now it was the spark that crackled through him and set him moving in strides towards her, arms outstretched, a thundering in his head, moving forward, knowing with all his body that nothing, nothing at all in this world, nothing could stop them now.

He was dimly aware that as he pressed her back, back, she cried out, "Leif, Leif, don't ever let that Dannto touch me! I love you, and only you!"

Later, like conscience knocking, knuckles tapped the door to the suite. Halla sat upright, eyes wide, mouth a scarlet O, unconsciously pulling the sheet up to her neck. Leif put his finger to his lips and tiptoed to a closet. Reaching it, he turned and made signs for her to answer. Then he pulled out his automatic.

He could, he reasoned, brazen his way out. It was his right as a lamechian doctor to examine a woman without a gapt being present. On the other hand, it would be better if it weren't known he'd been locked up so long with her. What he did depended upon the knocker's identity.

Halla called, "Who is it?"

The reply was the muffled voice of a man. Halla repeated her question. Slightly louder, the words

were still too low. Halla rose and put on her dressing
gown and went through two rooms to the door. Leif
followed her and stood behind her. This time they
both heard.

"Halla, this is Jake Candleman. Let me in."

The two raised their eyebrows. Leif nodded at her
to do so. Then he went back into the closet. Halla,
after asking the Uzzite to wait until she was back in
bed, turned off some of the lights and crawled under
the sheets.

As he'd purposefully left the closet door half-
open, Leif could see between its inner edge and the
wall. Candleman came into view, long body bent for-
wards as if there were a weak spot in its middle,
narrow face hard and cragged as a cliff. He strode up
to the bed and stopped, looked keenly around, and
then, to the consternation of both watchers, sank to
his knees by her side.

"Halla! Halla!" he crooned. "Forgive me,
Halla!"

She shrank away from his reaching hands.

"What do you mean? Forgive you for what?"

"You know what, Halla, dear. Don't tease, like
you used to do. I can't stand it. I won't. You know
you can't trifle with me. You know."

Her voice trembled as much as his. She said, "Are
you crazy? I haven't the slightest idea what you're
talking about."

He clutched one of her hands before she could get
it away.

"Don't tell me that! That's what you used to say
when I asked you where I could meet you again. You
made a madman out of me. I couldn't touch you
again, and yet I couldn't stand not to. I told you I'd
kill you, and I almost did. Halla, darling, tell me you
forgive me. I'll never do anything like that again. I
almost died myself when they said you'd been killed
at once in that wreck. When I found out you were

only slightly hurt, I raged and smashed the furniture in my apartment and swore I'd see you were dead for sure the next time.

"And yet, I was glad because you'd not been killed. I couldn't stand the thought. No more Halla. No Halla, no Halla, no Halla. My brain repeated over and over again, no Halla, no Halla."

The woman looked stupefied. Leif hoped she'd catch on to what was happening. Otherwise, she'd give herself away.

Candleman tried to pull her to him; she bent away, turning her face sideways.

"What's the matter with you?" he cried. "You're not so pure. You gave yourself to me once, remember? You betrayed your husband, a Sandalphon. I dishonored him and all he stands for. But I thought it worth it. Halla, there never was anybody like you, You and I . . ."

Leif could not believe the man's incoherent babbling. Candleman's voice, always so dead, rose and plunged; his face, usually hard and expressionless as a closed fist, twisted and writhed like a deaf-mute's fingers.

Leif saw now that it had been Candleman who had gotten the original Halla into a taxi, perhaps for one last rendezvous, and then had arranged the 'accident.' No wonder the man had been so suspicious about the minor injuries reported by Leif. He must have thought that Halla had reported him. Or else he'd wanted to get into her hospital room to finish her off. The chances were that he'd not been too scared of her talking, for she'd implicate herself. Moreover, he was a lamechian; he could do no wrong.

His main reason for trying to kill her was revenge. That was evident.

As Leif listened to Candleman talk and at the same time try to embrace Halla, he saw the pattern.

Evidently the dead woman had once felt sorry for him and had given in to him. Or perhaps she'd done it to find out something or to secure a favor she desperately needed. No one would ever know. Whatever the reason, she had refused to have any more to do with him after that one time. And he, finally convinced she loathed him, had tried to kill her. Not tried—he *had* done it. And the woman he was talking to must realize that and must hate him.

"Listen to me!" panted the Uzzite. "I told Dannto I was coming back to keep an eye on you, that I was still worried about assassins. It'll be hours before he and the other hunters return."

"What about Dr. Barker?" said Halla, straining to keep his face from hers.

"That lecher! He wouldn't dare bother us. For the sake of Sigmen, Halla, don't fight me so! I can't help myself; I *must* have you. I know you really want me. Otherwise, you'd never have acted the way you did that one time. You're just bothered by your unreal conduct. Halla, how do we know what is real and what is not?"

Leif hoped she could handle him, for he didn't want to be forced to reveal himself. If he hadn't been in love with her, he would have allowed Candleman to have his way. Halla was a CWC agent. That would only have been in line of duty. But he knew that he couldn't stand the Uzzite's pawing her much more.

"Please, Halla! I'll never try to kill you again."

"You beast," she said. "You were the one that loosed that Gemman at me."

"Forgive me, Halla. It won't happen again."

Suddenly, he stood up and seized her wrists and bent them back and leaned forward and placed his mouth against hers. Leif started to step out, but he paused when the man yelped with pain and jumped back from her. His lower lip was bleeding where she had clamped down upon it.

"You always did bite, Halla," he said. "But not too hard next time, please."

How blind could you get? wondered Leif. Another thought struck. Candleman had even covered up by using his favorite bugaboo: J.C. He'd had that pseudo-Neanderthal tattooed with those initials to confuse anybody who might possibly read them. Everybody was getting in on the game.

Halla stood up and said, "If you don't leave at once, I'll scream, and I'll get a gun and shoot you. Don't think I wouldn't."

Not a bad idea, thought Leif. That would solve many problems.

He raised his automatic and aimed at the high and narrow forehead, now covered with sweat.

Before he could pull the trigger, he heard a gentle tapping upon the suite-door.

Halla called out, "Who is it?"

Candleman brushed his hair back and wiped his face with a handkerchief and put his cap back on Then he strode towards the door, bent forward more than ever, as if the hinge in the middle of his body had broken.

He thrust his frequency-finder key into the lock, pressed the button, and opened the door.

Ava stepped in, said, "Pardon me, Chief," and went on.

The Uzzite did not look back but slammed the door behind him.

Leif came out from behind the closet door. "What're you doing back here?" he said to Ava.

"This!"

Ava handed him a comic, the latest issue of the *Adventures of the Forerunner*.

"Where'd you find it?"

"In my pocketbook. One of the guides must be CWC. It contains a message on the third page."

Leif opened it to the third page and read the words

underlined in a balloon above one of the characters.

"All *get under* the bridge. Stand your *ground* if the evil *Back*runner sees us. *Two* of you re*pair* this gun as *fast* as you can."

"All H must be breaking loose," said Leif. "What happened? Trausti talked? They caught Jim Crew? Zack Roe? Or something unexpected?"

Discussion was useless. There was nothing they could do about getting back unless they could find a reasonable excuse. At the moment, none was available. So they had to pass the next two days in Canada.

Ava fretted at the delay and became even more disturbed because Leif was not that anxious. He, on the contrary, hiked through the woods and fished. He wasn't going to sit around with tensed muscles and tight lips.

Much as he would have liked to take Halla along with him, he could not do so without exciting dangerous comment. He did find it possible to go fishing with her the second afternoon when he invited her and a couple of other hierarchs' wives along. While the women were unpacking the picnic luncheon, Leif managed a few words with Halla. His curiosity about certain things he'd discovered during the dissection of the original Halla was still driving him.

Halla answered his question calmly and entirely unself-consciously.

"Then that is why you make such a good agent for the CWC in this particular society?" said Leif.

"Yes," she answered. "The repression of normal sex impulses, the deliberate creation of frigidity in men and women, results in psychic castration. Tyrants long ago found out they could control their subjects much more easily if they set up a system, enforced by taboos instilled at an early age, that crushed the development of the human being as a whole. Quenching of wholesome relations between the sexes is an integral part of the Jack system.

"To put it briefly, psychically impotent people, by which I mean preverted people of any kind, by which I mean those not normal . . ."

She halted in confusion and laughed. "Actually, all I know is that the type of repression you find in the Union fulfills the function of keeping men more easily in submissiveness. You can find your parallel in geldings. They make more willing beasts of burden.

"But if, say, one of these men were to find a woman whose responses did not go by the books he'd read or the lectures he'd heard, a woman who possessed an organ that would automatically release those inhibitions and make him a free man for the first time in his unhappy and confused life, then he'd value that woman and keep her, even if he had to do so secretly and in defiance of the mores. You follow me?"

"Pretty much so," he said, glancing around to see if any of the hierarchs' wives were in earshot. "Frigidity in a man results in what we call a muscular armor, a contraction of the pelvic floor. The armor is a result of the neurosis. The psyche deliberately causes the soma to use muscular rigidity and squeezing to inhibit itself. But, curiously enough, if the muscular armor can be relaxed, then the neurosis quite often lessens or goes away. The man, freed in one part of his development as a complete human being, also gains liberty in other fields. That is, he laughs more, thinks more deeply, is more sincere and yet is at the same time gayer, is even freer of psychosomatic diseases, and so on. You know what I mean."

"Yes. Take my husband, Dannto, for instance. He used to be almost as gloomy and hostile as

Candleman. Now, though he's a long way to go as a desirable individual, he's much jollier and broader-minded than before he met me. He doesn't realize it, consciously, but he wouldn't allow me to leave him for any reason."

"Correct me if I'm wrong," said Leif. "The bio-electrical current from the organ that was put into you stimulates the parasympathetic nervous system. This results in the uninhibiting of the muscular armor and the consequent momentary freedom from the anxiety feeling. The floodgates are opened; there is no damming up of emotion and its consequent stagnation into a cesspool. Am I right?"

"Yes; And the men are quite grateful. We gain an enormous hold ever them—to the profit of the world and the loss of the Haijac Union."

Leif had several more questions which he had to have answered.

"You and your sister were twins," he said. "But your retina prints and your fingerprints should have been different. Yet they were identical."

"The March biologists removed one of my sister's eye-balls. Using it as a pattern, they grew two duplicates. They replaced my sister's eyeball, removed mine, and implanted the duplicates in me. To make my fingerprints identical to my sister's they stripped the skin from my fingers and grew new skin, again using my sister's patterns as a blueprint."

"And the rudimentary antennae on your head and nerve cables connecting them with your brain?"

"They're the result of an unsuccessful experiment," she said. "My sister and I are—were—the only agents equipped with them. We were supposed to be able to transmit and receive brain waves through the antennae. As a matter of fact, we could. But the waves meant nothing to us. They were just so much static. We needed some biological device to filter out the 'noise.' The scientists left the antennae on us while they worked to perfect a filter. As far as I know, they haven't found one yet.''

Leif grinned and said, ''So there goes my theory you two were of extra-Terrestrial orgin. Too much imagination on my part—and too little knowledge of what my own country was doing in science!''

Chapter 20

ON THE FOLLOWING evening Dannto, Halla, Leif, Ava and several others got into a Paris-bound coach.

Candleman was not with them; he had left two hours after the scene in the bedroom. Business was his plea for leaving, but Leif suspected he didn't want to ride with Halla.

Their trip was quick and pleasant except for one puzzling event. Leif noticed that Ava had gone into the women's room for just a moment. On coming out, Ava was very pale. Leif had no chance to ask what the matter was, but he thought Ava must have received a message from a CWC-agent. That disturbed him. As Ava's superior, he should have gotten it. However, it might have been that the setup was such that Ava could be reached easier than he. Or Ava might have, not a message, but a stomach-ache.

When the coach slid into the Paris field, Dannto reminded the others they were to come at 1900 to his home for a party. The occasion would be a celebration over his wife's quick recovery following the

accident. Dannto seemed to be very happy. He
laughed and waved his hands as he told jokes. Halla
was not so radiant. She looked at Leif meaningfully,
and her eyes told him what kind of celebration Dannto was planning later that night.

For the first time since he'd been a very young
man, Leif was jealous. He felt sick. He also felt like
getting up and hitting the Sandalphon in the nose.

The rest of the trip the red-haired beauty glanced
now and then at him. Once he thought he saw the
beginnings of tears in her eyes.

He was sure of it when she excused herself and
went to the women's room, and stayed there a long
time.

Later, after all had disembarked and gone their
ways, Leif said to Ava, "Why so pale, pretty
maiden?"

Ava snarled back at him, and he decided it was
sickness, not a communication, that had made Ava
look so ill. Both were silent until the taxi brought
them to the hospital.

Leif was looking for notes from Rachel or Roe
when Ava came in, paler than ever.

"Did you find anything on the kymos?" Leif
asked.

Ava extended a shaking hand in which was a
graph. He took it and read the recordings of Zack
Roe's semantic waves. Sigur, the assistant, had
obeyed Leif's instructions and placed all the eegie
work done during his absence in a special file. Ava
had picked out the one with the message.

He read, and he paled. When he looked up, he saw
the automatic in Ava's hand.

"You're the executioner?" he asked unbelievingly.

Ava's voice trembled. "No, I'm only the escort."

"And very prettily armed, too," said Leif,
recovering his poise. "Well, when does this
drumhead take place?"

"Leif," Ava said, "I hate to do this. We've worked together so long. But orders are orders. And you shouldn't have let that . . . that woman go to your head. How could you have put us all in jeopardy by deliberately disobeying the command to cremate that girl at once? And then making love to the other?"

"So you did inform on me?" he said, gritting his teeth.

"It was my duty."

"Hating Halla didn't have anything to do with it, heh? Or was it hate? Did you have designs on her, too?"

"That's neither here nor there," Ava replied. "Come on, Leif. If I put this gun away, will you promise not to try a break?"

"All right. You're still enough of a soldier. I suppose."

Ava went to a closet and pulled some garments from the false bottom of a dirty clothes hamper.

"Here. Put these on."

He examined them. "So it's that bad, is it? We're through here."

"Yes. The thoughtpicker isn't in the eegie. Leif. Our men must have moved it away sometime today when the word came."

Ava undressed and began putting on the blues of the unskilled laborer. "Lord, Leif, it'll be good looking like a man again! Ten years of pretending to be a female!"

"You gave up a lot for the Service," he answered. "Tell me, Ava, honey, was it worth it?"

"Any more of that, and I *will* shoot you," she—he—said.

Leif had become so accustomed to Avam Soski posing as his wife that he seldom thought of him in terms of his true sex. The little fellow was good, one of the greatest disguise-men in the CWC.

Leif dressed, walked to the QB and flicked it on.

Ava said, "None of that. Orders are that you communicate with nobody."

He ignored him and asked the autoperator for Mrs. Dannto's room. She should be getting ready for the party. If the Sandalphon were with her, his presence wouldn't matter. They had arranged a code word.

"Leif, I'll shoot!" cried Ava.

The cube showed Halla coming into the front room of her suite. She was in a robe.

"Halla, is there anybody else to hear?" he asked.

She shook her head and stared past him at Ava's leveled gun.

"Don't worry," he said. "Ava won't shoot. Listen! The jig is up. I haven't time to go into detail. The gist is that we're getting out of here. I can't tell you how, because this line may be monitored. I don't think so; both you and I get automatic lamechian privileges; but you never know. Just meet me where we agreed to. Fast! Got it?"

She nodded her head again, and he cut them off.

Swinging around on Ava, Leif said, "I'm not going with you, baby. I intend to contact Jim Crew and get him to ship Halla and me to Bantuland."

"Jim Crew is in H," said Ava flatly. He held his gun steady on Leif's chest.

"When did you learn that? In the women's room on the coach?"

"Yes. Roe told us to get under because he thinks the Uzzites will torture the truth from Crew. I think the 'picker has been moved close to H so Roe can listen in on the ordeal."

Leif hesitated and said, "Ava, listen. I know you'll shoot me if I drive you too far. But what about giving me a break? What do you say you take both Halla and myself to the drumhead? I can make a plea that

Roe let us go. I'm no use to CWC any more; killing me won't help him."

"Do you think that after you've messed up the Halla replacement and gotten involved with the Bantus and talked Halla into abandoning her post that Roe'll pardon you? Leif, that girl has gone to your head!"

"I know it."

"But, Leif—betraying your country?"

"I didn't. I just forgot it for the moment."

They walked out of the hospital. Leif took his personal car and drove to the front of the National Library. Halla was waiting inside. She walked out and got into the seat behind the two men.

Before Ava could tell Leif where to go, Halla pulled a gun from her purse and stuck it against the little man's neck. Leif reached over and removed Ava's automatic from his pocket.

"I could see what was coming," he said. "So Halla and I made our plans, too."

Ava seemed stunned. "Leif, this isn't . . . isn't . . ."

"Like me? Perhaps not. But I took one wrong step and that led me to the next. Not that meeting Halla was wrong. I wouldn't pass that up for all the medals in the world. The thing is, the CWC would consider me disloyal from the first. I have no choice. Understand this—I'm not turning against March. After this is over, I'll volunteer for a trial there, when emotions have cooled down some. But right now I'd get shot."

Fighting the savage desire to race pell-mell down the streets and take corners on two wheels, Leif drove slowly and carefully to a subway entrance close to the square that had once enclosed the Arc de Triomphe. They got out, and Leif put the car on auto for the hospital.

He took one look at the four-hundred-foot statue of Sigmen, holding a sword and an hourglass, had a vagrant thought as to what successor to the Arc and the Forerunner would someday stand there, and then followed Ava and Halla down into a subway and from thence into the tunnels that would lead to the hideout of the Bantus.

They rode to a spot four blocks from their destination, and walked the rest of the way. The meeting-place was a room in a house for lower-class workers. It was on one side of a very large square. Far on the other side was a huge block-like building that was, supposedly, a college for psych techs.

Actually, it was H.

The three approached the roominghouse from the rear, walked up three flights of rickety steps, down a hall stinking of cabbage and fish and sweat, and to a room that fronted the square. Ava tapped the code; the door opened; they stepped in.

"Where's Roe?" said Ava.

The man gestured at the empty room and said, "He's hiding. So is about half of the Corps. Candleman's found out what we're doing. He left me here so I could warn anyone who came to the drumhead."

Curiously, he looked at the guns Halla and Leif held in their hands, but made no comment.

"What about Barker?" said Ava.

"He's to hide like the rest of us. Get away as best he can. Roe will deal with him later."

Halla sighed with relief.

Leif said, "Well, I did my best. From now on, if he wants me, he'll have to come and get me."

He walked up to the 'picker which was standing by a closed windowblind and said, "Is it set to explode?"

The man replied, "Not unless somebody tries to

open it. I was using it on Jim Crew. They're giving him a hell of a treatment over there.''

Leif clucked and shook his head. He knew that in every one of these buildings scattered through the Union, the "unreal" thinkers were reconverted to reality.

There techs drugged the subjects, laid them on couches, and attached minute synapse-wires to various nerve-endings. Through these they fed a series of stimuli that created the sensations the techs desired. These, coordinated with words whispered by a recording, made the subject live artificial situations which he thought were actual happenings. The "story" was repeated over and over, until it was stamped unalterably for life upon the subject's being, until it had all the unconscious authority of a conditioned-reflex.

Released from H, the subject was convinced that he had gone through an experience that had shown him the error of his ways. Thereafter, he was an unquestioning citizen. No matter what his beliefs before his entrance into H, he was now a loyal disciple of Isaac Sigmen.

The one disadvantage was that he no longer could think creatively. He was as close to being an automation as a person could be.

Leif knew this. Peering into Crew's mind would be distressing, but an impulse he couldn't fight made him turn on the 'picker and put on the ear phones. These latter gave him the auditory translations of the "semantic" waves radiating from the Bantu's cortex.

Chapter 21

LEIF TOOK TWENTY minutes to find Jim Crew's brainwave pattern. His beam probed here and there, stabbed up and down corridors and into rooms where techs sat, metal helmets on heads, watching dials, running tapes and making records. Wires from their helmets and various instruments pierced the walls and ran to the bodies of the subjects. Each wire ended in an exceedingly fine network that connected with this or that nerve-plexus. Through these techs were feeding the pre-set stimuli that gave the subjects their illusions.

Leif, of course, could not see anything within the building, but he could visualize it because of what he'd been told about H and because of thoughts he caught from those techs whose heads weren't shielded by the impenetrable metal caps.

The men working on Jim Crew had a beautifully evil situation for him, one that followed the pattern of his own thinking. Leif tapped the Bantu's semantic-waves just as they were beginning the story for the first or hundredth time. He was at a loss to understand it, but in a short time he began inserting his own interpretations in the inevitable gaps and static. He was helped by the fact that the man was sub-vocalizing much of what he was undergoing, just as a man talks in his sleep.

The subject was awakened from a sound sleep by a gentle voice whispering over and over, "Jim Crew, open your eyes. Jim Crew, don't cry out."

And when he did so, or, rather, thought he did, he saw a man standing in the corner of his cell. The stranger was black-skinned and naked and had a face that was Jim Crew's own, though the features were somewhat etherealized. He looked as Jim Crew would have liked to look.

Jim wasn't too surprised at seeing this visitor. He had always know that sooner or later he would come. He calmly accepted the obviousness of his having walked through the wall. He was, however, thrilled to see a shimmering nimbus around the close-cut hair.

"Come, Jim Crew," the man said. "I am here to take you away, far from these people who know not what they do."

As if in a dream, Jim floated to his feet and seized the hand held out to him. It was large and strong and warm with a power Jim had never felt before, not even when he'd hold hands in the big tribal dances and the whirling circles had created power for healing and for understanding and love.

This was an energy that flowed to him as the higher potential flows to the lower. This was the source of that power that he'd dreamed about and sometimes seen in his prayers when he was alone or had glimpsed, oh so briefly, at the climax of a great dance.

Child-like, Jim took the hand and followed the man through the wall and felt not a tinge of fear when the brief darkness closed around him. Then he was through the cement, and he was rising in the air, borne upwards by the power of the hand. Below him, Paris was spread out in night and in clusters and strings of glowpearls, and then it dwindled and grew small and the curve of the earth was far off and the air grew colder. A warmth spread out from the man like a robe, and though Jim Crew shivered at the first stroke of the fingers of space he quickly enough forgot about it.

They were poised between earth and moon with Jim Crew gazing curiously at the moon, for in this day where men rode to the stars, he had never left the atmosphere, thinking that this planet was big enough and beautiful enough for what he wanted to do in his life.

The man with the head like a saintly Jim Crew's said, "Look! You have been faithful to your Master, and so I reward you with this."

And he gestured at all of Earth and the moon and the stars.

Jim Crew cried out, "But, Lord, this isn't what I want!"

His words fell out into dark space and froze and hurtled like cold iron towards the globe below, and when they struck the air they burned and sent out long tails of flame and released their content so that he hard his voice, firestreaked and amplified in the vast bowl of Earth, coming back at him, mockingly and somehow distorted, "But Lord, this isn't what I want!"

And the man said, "But what do you want? What else is there but this?"

And when Jim Crew turned to look at him, for the meaning and the tones chilled him as space itself had not done, he saw that the man's face was as wise and kind and loving as before. But he also saw that the voice came from another's mouth, and when he looked into the eyes that went with that mouth, he felt for the first time in his life a Fear. This head was his too, and it was what Jim Crew had hoped he would never become, for there was evil stamped so deeply into it that it would never come out.

And when the twisted mouth, wicked, yet his as much as was the mouth of the man who'd rescued him, repeated, "But what else is there?" Jim Crew squeezed upon the man's hand for all the power he could absorb. But the man had turned partly sidewise, and Jim could see that he had grown a long thick tail that stuck up behind him like a saucy monkey's. Upon its end, as if the tail were a neck, was the head of the twisted-mouth Jim Crew. When it saw that Jim understood, it laughed and said, "Did you really think there was anything beyond that, Jim Crew, beyond those hard hot and cold globes drifting aimlessly through infinity and eternity? Did you really believe in a Something else?"

Jim Crew cried out and tried to jerk away and run on the nothingness beneath his feet, for the hand holding his had grown icy and was sucking power from his body, and the head that had been what Jim wanted to be was melting like a hot candle and changing features.

But he could not run, for he was sprawled out on the bosom of space, great breasts that offered no sustenance and no love, and though he frantically rowed hands and kicked feet, he moved nowhere.

And then the two-headed man had placed a foot like a talon upon his back and sent him down with a shove that made the universe reel. He fell and left space and struck the air as if it were the surface of the sea and slowed and then fell faster again as the air whistled by and the earth came up as if thrown at him. His skin began burning because he was a meteor of flesh now and would go up flames and smoke and agony long before he struck.

He shouted, "Lord, surely none of your martyrs ever burned before in such a manner!"

And no sooner had the words left him than he became aware of a hand that gripped his shoulder and slowed him down so that the flaming air cooled and he drifted gently. When he looked up, he saw that the man who had saved him had the red hair and narrow bright-blue eyes and big vulture's beak of Isaac Sigmen, the Forerunner.

His voice was that of the dove.

"Now that you have been betrayed by the one you thought was your master, and now you have seen that there is nothing beyond the palpable, and now you have been saved by the true prophet, the traveler in time, founder of the Sturch that will save all men, surely you must see what a lie you have been living in and how you must work with the followers of the Forerunner to remedy your misdirected labors to make reality into pseudo-time."

And though Jim Crew knew that what he was experiencing was that which *was*—for he could see and feel and hear—he still knew that he was being tempted in a subtle manner that none of his fellows had ever faced.

He turned and wrested himself from the Forerunner's grasp and breathed deeply and shouted, "Master, wherever you are, come now, or I am lost!"

The next moment Leif Barker's ears were filled with such a crackling of static he had to tear off his ear phones. But he found that it did no good, for something had reached him from the building across the street and plunged deep into him in a manner that was shattering. A light, blinding, explosive, so filled him that he could see nothing else. He fell backwards upon the floor and did not hear Ava and Halla when they yelled, or feel them when they lifted him up.

Then, in the next second, the light was gone, and he was back in the world he knew.

Ignoring their questions or protests, Leif rose, shook his head, and put the ear phones back on. He found what he's expected. Jim Crew's brainwaves no longer existed.

He switched to a searchbeam and centered upon the head of a tech who had taken his helmet off and had run into the room where the Bantu lay beneath his cocoon of wires. As the tech was vocalizing, Leif had no trouble understanding.

The man was saying, as reported by his semantic waves, "I don't know what happened! He was responding the way he should have. He'd just reached that part of the record where the Forerunner was telling him he'd been betrayed. Then, just like that, the needles on our dials shot over to full, staying there a second, and then fell to zero! He must have been pouring out a super-human amount of energy! Much more than I would have thought possible!"

Leif poked his beam around the room until he picked up another man.

"He's dead. What killed him? Heart attack?"

Another replied, "He doesn't look as if he died of a heart attack. Look at the smile on his face. What in Sigmen's name could he have been thinking of?"

That was enough for Leif. He removed the phones and said to the others in room, "Let's get out of here. I'll tell you about it later."

The man who had admitted them to the room refused to go back with them into the subway. He had another place to hole up. After hesitating, Ava, however, said he would go with Leif and Halla. The three left at once. They didn't bother with the thoughtpicker. When the Uzzites tried to open it, it would explode.

Leif seemed preoccupied. As they went down the

rickety steps of the boardinghouse, he was muttering, "I was the only one around who was in any kind of contact with Jim, even if it was just mental sympathy. The techs couldn't see what he was thinking. They were just feeding him a prepared story and watching his reactions on meters.

"But when that . . . vision . . . came to him, I saw part if it. Not through the 'picker but directly. Energy, mental or otherwise, flows from a higher charged body to a lesser if there is a conductor. Our first connection was the machine and our second was our sympathy. And of the two of us I was the lesser charged."

He shook his head as if to throw out something that clung leechlike.

"Somehow, I saw what he saw. I'm sure it wasn't real, not as this flesh and blood that surround my bones are real. The mind works in signs and symbols, and Jim Crew's whole being was summed up in that last flare of energy, that psychosomatic nova. What he, and I, witnessed was a symbol he projected to himself. It was . . . essence, not existence."

He shook his head again and mumbled, "But who was that dark and bearded man stepping through the light, holding out his hand to Jim? *Was* there a man, or did I just think I saw . . .?"

And he ran his hand through his hair and tugged at the roots and knew that, though he could explain it away, he would never be sure.

Chapter 22

IN THE HIDE-OUT of the Bantus, two watchers
met them and conducted them through the darkness.
Ava had started to protest that he didn't want to go
along, but Leif had told him that he was forcing him.
If both disappeared, Roe might think they'd been
arrested and sent to H. If Ava took the news to him
of what had happened, Roe might put obstacles in
Leif's path. Once the man and the woman were on
the ship to Africa, Ava could go.

When they arrived, they greeted the Primitives and
then were fed. A parley was held; its result was the
agreement that an exodus to a new HQ would have to
be set up. Meanwhile, Leif and several others would
go to the ship. They were lucky, for in one more day
the vessel would leave, and another one wouldn't be
in for a month.

Prayers were offered for Jim Crew after the meal.
Leif and Halla chafed, though they appreciated the
sentiment. And then, about three in the morning,
just as they were to leave, a watcher came in. His face
was twisted with alarm and with bad news.

Candleman and Dannto knew now that Halla had run away with Barker. The Uzzite had launched the biggest manhunt of them all, one he'd been preparing for a long time and that was ready to move when he was stung into action.

He was not only using all of his Parisian force, but had borrowed thousands from surrounding areas. They had dogs and firethrowers and poison gases.

Leif talked to some of the watchers. They said the Uzzite chief had tried to bring in his men quietly and under cover of night, but it was impossible to conceal that number, especially from the supersensitive Bantus. It would be some time before the hunters reached the vicinity of their hideout. Candleman had started from the periphery with a huge army that would close in towards the center. The idea was that the underground dwellers would be driven like rabbits in a big beat.

Leif didn't think it would be that easy. Paris was tremendous, twice as large as the twentieth century city, and the labyrinth beneath was many leveled and tortuous. It would be several days before the hunters even got close to the Bantus, and it would be impossible for individuals to slip through the lines.

There was another council. The Bantus hoped they would be able to think of some place to go above ground while the hunt was on.

Leif killed that hope by telling them that Uzzites would also be prowling the streets and subways now in use for just such a maneuver. There were only two things to do. One, hope they'd not be found. Or, two, take the ship that rested in the mud at the bottom of the Seine. The first was rather hopeless; once found they'd have no chance to escape. The second was dangerous, for there was no way of knowing whether or not Candleman had tortured the truth from Jim Crew about the ship. It was probable that he had.

Leif's own advice was to take the ship. He hoped he and Halla could live for a while in Bantuland, that perhaps he could begin negotiations for reinstatement in March. If that proved hopeless, the two of them could either remain in Africa or go to one of the Israeli Republics.

The family members scanned each other for the general feeling. There was no question of splitting up. They either stayed as a unit or left as one. Leif, watching them, could not help thinking that here was a democracy undereamed of. No votes had to be cast, no ballots written, no speeches, no bribing, no appeals to emotional issues. They held hands, though it wasn't necessary, and *felt* their way to a decision.

The whole thing took less than a minute. Unanimously, they agreed to go. If they were to stay, their martyrdom would mean nothing, for the people of the Haijac would not see and benefit by it. It was true that once they left Paris it would be very difficult to get back in. But it could be done. Besides, they had great confidence that the plans of the Marchers would eventually succeed and that the Haijac would fall.

Preparations got underway at once. Clothes were put on and food stored in baskets. Within twenty minutes, the whole group was ready.

Leif asked about the Timbuktumen and was told they had lost contact with them ever since they'd offended Dr. Djouba. Doubtless, unless they, too, had very good avenues of escape, they would be flushed out and killed or sent to H.

A watcher entered breathlessly and said that a number of men had come underground through the entrance in the lavatory wall, the very place which Leif and Crew had used the first time. Another watcher came in after the first to say that a second party was coming from the opposite direction.

"Evidently they're going to try to grind us between

them," said Leif. He strode through a door into the room whose wall concealed an exit. They planted a bomb and set it to be triggered by the brainwaves of the fourth person to enter the room.

Leif, Ava, and Halla were the only ones of the hunted who were armed; the Bantus would rather die than have the blood of others on their hands.

When Leif walked by the others on his way back to the head of the line, he passed Anadi, the child on whom he'd operated. Pale but brighteyed, she was being carried in the arms of one her fathers. Her face seemed small compared to the big white basketwork enclosing her skull. He slowed for a second to accompany her.

"Anadi, it's hard to believe you're alive."

"Yes," she answered, smiling feebly. "I stayed alive so I might die with all of us."

He didn't ask her what she meant; it was obvious.

He said, "I've been too busy to find out just why you happened to be at the scene of the first Halla's death. Tell me, what did Jim Crew mean when he said you knew she was going to be in an accident? And that you'd be hurt, and I'd save you?"

"How can I explain? I knew Mrs. Dannto because I was the first one who converted her to our faith. I loved her; I baptised her."

"Ah, if the CWC had known that, it'd have court-martialed her, too."

"Yes, But that day she was killed, I had a *feeling* that she was making a move she shouldn't. I hurried to warn her, but I was too late. I was in the way; the taxi drove over me. As for you, we found out who you really were a long time ago."

He touched her hand and, for some reason, felt stronger.

"You're a strange little girl."

"Not half as strange as you are, Lev-Leif Baruch-Barker."

That was the last time he saw her . . .

They threaded very narrow tunnels with low roofs. Leif had to help Halla at several places, for the ceilings or sides had caved in and partially blocked them.

At one of them, they paused as a low rumble came from behind and the ground shook.

"The bomb!" remarked Leif grimly. "There'll be more along soon. But they'll be cautious."

Presently they came to a broad room, an excavation shored up in many places by timbers and stone pillars. There the Africans insisted the three agents take another tunnel. If the hunters caught up, they said, they could at least delay them while the three went on to the ship. As for the group, it would live or die as a unit.

Leif didn't argue. He wanted to live. He was surprised, however, when the girl he's thought of as Brindled Beatrice said she'd leave the others to guide. He was touched, for he knew it was because of her feeling for him that she was sundering herself from the group, a gesture which was almost like tearing off her flesh.

Leif said, "Thank you. This is a great sacrifice on your part."

"Not so much. We'll meet again at the ship."

It was then that Leif got the feeling that they would *not* meet the others, that the group had decided, with their soundless balloting, that the hunters would probably catch them and that they could, at least, give their lives for the two men and woman. Beatrice had been informed of this.

The four took the tunnel to the right. They had gone a hundred yards when they heard the distant barking of dogs and shouting of men. They hurried on, knowing that soon enough the pursuers would be on their heels.

When they slowed down because Halla was reeling

from the pace, they stopped for a second at the juncture, of four tunnels and heard, dimly, the firing of many guns.

Beatrice stiffened and cried out, "They're killing us! They're not giving us a chance!"

She put her head on Leif's chest and wept. He patted her bare back and said, "There's nothing to be done. Let's go, or we'll be caught, too."

Sobbing, the girl turned and trotted on.

Halla, in the lead, suddenly fell. Before she could rise, she screamed. Leif leaped at the man lying on the ground, ready to shoot him, when he saw he was wounded and a Bantu. He put his automatic down and was going to help the man when he understood why she had been so frightened.

He was one of the Men In The Dark.

Injured as he was, with blood flowing from a shoulder-wound, he was still able to catch Halla's mindimages, amplify them, and hurl them back. As fear was uppermost in her mind, he'd probably shown her something that had really terrified her.

Beatrice bent over him and said, "Come along, brother. We'll help you."

Drooling, lips hanging open, blue eyes staring into the roots of Beatrice's mind, he staggered to his feet and followed her.

Leif wanted to protest, for he thought the presence of a crazy and wounded man would hinder them. Moreover, the fellow's essence was evil. Let him die. Beatrice, however, had put her arm around him and was helping him along. Watching her, Leif felt ashamed that he'd allowed his fear to overcome him and tried to excuse himself by saying he was more worried about Halla than anything. But he had to admit to himself he was rationalizing. It had been the brutal panic of the beast in flight that had affected him.

The clamor behind them was getting louder. They

came to another junction. Beatrice halted them.

"From here on," she said, "Take every other exit on the right. Got it? First left, then right. They left, then right."

Leif said, "If you've some fantastic notion of staying here and luring them down another tunnel, forget it. We'll stick together."

"I'm half dead now," she replied. "When my people died, I died. So it's only a little step to join them. You go on. You can't stop me."

Barker didn't hesitate. He embraced her and said, "We'll never forget you, Beatrice—and—*we* love you."

"You'll find me a million times over in Bantuland," she said. "I'll live in all my people."

Leif didn't believe that, but despite himself he was overwhelmed. He turned and said, "Let's go."

Ava and Halla touched the splotched skin of the girl and then followed him. The Man In The Dark hung his head for a moment, muttered something in Swahili, and staggered off after the three.

Beatrice waited for the hounds . . .

Ten minutes later, Leif knew that she must as least have split the party that was tracking them. He caught a glimpse of the comparatively small group as they came down a very long subway route. There was one dog and twenty men. Candleman's thin bent-forward figure and Dannto's hogfat body were side by side in the lead. In the brief glimpse he got of them before he ducked through an archway, he saw that most of them carried the minimatics which could spray hundreds of slugs, without stopping to cool off. Each one of the bullets was explosive and would blow a hole an inch wide and an inch deep in the flesh of a man.

Leif had his own weapon, but he didn't want to let the trackers know they were close. He ran to join the others and found that Halla was limping. In reply to his alarmed questions, she said she'd hurt her ankle when she tripped over the Man In The Dark. She was trying to hide her pain, but both men could see she would soon be reduced to a hobble.

Leif put his arm around her waist and let her lean on him. They found that the hopping hurt her almost as much as the walking by herself did and that they could not go much faster.

He stopped and picked her up, despite her protests, and carried her in his arms. He was large and very strong, but she, too, was tall and no light weight and was bound to be a burden even to a Samson. Leif tried half-running, half-walking. He made good time. Not good enough, however, for the barking and shouting behind them increased in volume. Hampered as he was, he would inevitably be caught.

Ava said, "Stop, Leif."

Leif obeyed, for he was beginning to pant.

"What do you want?" he asked. The question was a cover-up. He knew well enough what Ava was going to do.

"I'll hold them as long as I can," said Ava. "You get a good head start, and I'll coming running later."

"Ava," said Leif, "You know there'll be no later."

Ava started to deny it, then shook his head and smiled slightly.

"You're right. But I look at it this way. I can't go to Africa. How would I prove I didn't desert my post and run with you? I'd be court-martialed and disgrace my wife and child and mother. If I die here, the CWC'll proclaim me a hero. I have to die, anyway. Better a dead hero than a dead traitor.

"You've something to live for, even though I wouldn't under any conditions touch that . . . that woman thing. So get going, Leif, and best of luck to you. I don't think you'll be happy with that woman, but she seems to be what you want."

Leif said, "I'm sorry you still persist in thinking of Halla that way. But it can't be helped. *Shalom*, Ava."

"If you're ever admitted back to March, Leif, see my son and wife. He's eleven now. Tell them I died well. *Shalom*."

Leif began to take off his wristbox to give to the little man. Ava refused it, saying Leif might have a better use for it. So the big man shrugged and picked Halla up and walked off without a backward look, though it hurt him to do so. The wounded Bantu lurched behind him.

Presently, somewhere for behind them, guns chattered. There was an almost continuous noise and then a vast, shattering roar.

"That'll be Ava's work," said Leif. "He must have blown himself up."

After a while, lights and shouts came. Leif, deciding he could not carry Halla any more, put her down behind a half-fallen wall of brick. The Bantu also flopped. In a few seconds, his harsh breathing had ceased. Leif was glad, because he'd been worrying about the fellow's mirror-mind. So far, he'd little effect, probably because he was too intent on his wound and partly because, as Leif had learned, those who had little to hide were not affected so much. Halla had very few inhibitions to bring up, very few unconscious hates. She laughted and wept and loved easily and openly. Such people did not have a dark rotten humus in their psyche.

Suddenly, men were shouting nearby. Leif aimed his minimatic at the party as they rounded a corner about twenty yards away. Two men fell; the others jumped back. He was disappointed because neither Candleman nor Dannto were among them, but he'd not expected them to be. Made cautious by their experience with Ava, they would send their men ahead to draw fire. It was satisfying to know they only had one man left to precede them.

The lights around the corner went out. That meant that the Jacks were either going to rush in the dark, which he doubted, or that they had Darklight beams and oggles. The latter were fine for lightless fighting, but their disadvantage was that if an enemy turned a flash on them while they were wearing the goggles, they couldn't see it.

Why should he wait for them? He and the other two could crawl away and take up another position. He gave the order; they did so, stopping around another corner about thirty yards down the tunnel.

Only a minute later, the tunnel was solid from one end to the other with a blinding light; a dazzlebomb. Had he stayed behind the wall, he would have been sightless.

Chapter 23

FOOTSTEPS POUNDED AS an Uzzite, holding a flash in one hand, ran to the wall, prepared to shoot down helpless victims. Leif waited until he was by the bricks, for he hoped the other two would follow. They didn't, so he killed the attacker, and, before the man collapsed, was up and running to him. His plan was to seize the flash, which was lying on the ground, and pretend he was the Uzzite himself. If he could get the two to step around the corner . . .

One did. Candleman. He shot first, and though Leif threw himself behind the wall, he felt the automatic blown out of his hand by the stream of tiny slugs. The weapon lay in front of the flash, where Candleman could see it.

Leif's hand was numb because the terrific force of the explosive bullet had communicated itself through the metal. He swore and held his wrist and felt helpless. He hoped Halla would shoot; no sooner the thought than the *brrrrrrp* of her automatic followed. Then it ceased, and her voice came, shrill and urgent,

"Leif, I didn't get him! He's on the other side of the wall!"

"If he sticks his head or hand out, shoot him!" he called back.

"Dannto!" yelled Candleman. "Barker has dropped his gun! Shoot out that flash so Halla can't see, and I'll get him!"

"When he does that, Halla," bellowed Leif, "turn on your light and pin him as he comes around the wall. Or over!"

Dannto must have dared to stick his hand around the corner, for his gun hosed the tunnel, feeling for the flash. As was inevitable, he hit it. However, when the light shattered, he did not stop, but kept shooting. He was trying to keep Halla from projecting her head from her corner. And he was being successful, for her beam did not flash on.

However, Candleman did not dare jump over the wall until Dannto was through firing.

Leif waited, knowing that the moment would come when even Dannto's seemingly inexhaustible clips would be empty. When that happened, the Uzzite would probably stick his arm over the bricks and hose the area where he'd seen Leif. Halla would flash the beam on; whatever happened then would be up to the faster of the two.

He inched up to the wall, keeping his head down to avoid the lethal swarm. When he reached the wall, he held the wristbox up to his mouth and spoke a code word. The ordered vibrations fractured a tiny disk inside the box. The disk had kept an equally tiny dial from being turned. Leif twisted the now free dial to the right and then flicked on the toggle that sent a predetermined frequency broadcasting from the box.

Dannto's gun stopped chattering. Silence, then a loud cry, full of fear and agony and despair.

"Halla!"

And silence again. Dannto was out of ammunition and out of breath—forever.

The coded word sent by Leif's box had stirred the ingredients left in Dannto's body during the operation for removal of his tumor. Mixed, the chemicals formed a poison that paralyzed him in one second and stopped his heart in another.

Leif had killed the Archurielite before the gun emptied because he knew that Candleman was familiar with their capacity and would be counting the seconds until it stopped. Whereupon the Uzzite, thinking himself safe from the fire of the obviously hysterical Dannto, would attack. The doctor hoped to jump first and catch Candleman off balance.

He rose and jumped to the top of the brick wall, close to the side of the tunnel. At the same time, Halla, inspired by some unlucky devil, turned her flash on and caught Leif dead center in it. If Candleman had asked for it, he couldn't have obtained a better target. He could have shot him off the wall as if he were a crow on a fence.

But Candleman outfoxed himself. He had rushed around the wall hoping to catch Leif offguard. He whirled to shoot the man on the wall; Leif kept on going and jumped down just as the Uzzite hosed where he had been. Candleman was fast-thinking, for he kept on revolving and shooting. He must have known that when Halla saw Leif on the wall, she had held her fire for fear of hitting him. Aware also that the agent had no gun, he decided in that second that the girl was the one to be taken care of.

Leif looked around the side of the wall to see Candleman's bent back turned to him, outlined in Halla's beam. The Uzzite's uniform had been blown apart; his coat hung on him in rags; his boots were ripped; his pants hung in shreds. A dark spot showed on his back. Leif, seeing all those details in an instant, guessed that the spot was a burn.

Then, as the doctor launched himself at the man's back, he saw the flash jump out of Halla's hand and roll back around the corner where it turned in upon her. Though it had been struck, the flash still shone, but evidently it was not being picked up again, for the beam remained motionless. Nor was there any fire from the woman.

Leif bellowed with agony and fury. Halla must have been hit; she must be dead!

The next instant, something struck his head. It was the Uzzite's pistol butt, coming down out of the darkness and driving Leif into an even deeper night.

Chapter 24

HE AWOKE FEELING as if an axe was buried in his skull. His hands were manacled in front of him; his back was against a cold damp wall. Halla sat across the tunnel. Her hands were cuffed also. A wing of dried blood across her face showed what had happened to knock her out. She'd been hit in the temple by a chip of brick knocked loose by an exploding bullet. That was bad, but he was happy that she had not been seriously hurt.

Candleman stood before Leif. He was shouting into a wristbox and obviously getting no answer. His flashlight was lying upon a shelf sticking out of the wall, its end propped up so it shone down upon them all.

Just inside the circle of light, a pair of naked and dirty feet pointed their toes to the roof. They belonged to the Man In The Dark. He must have been dead or near dead, for Leif could not discern any manacles restraining him.

Candleman quit giving orders into the box and said

to Leif, "So, Jacques Cuze, you've decided to come to life?"

Leif felt too sick to try to smile defiance. He said, "How did you find out who Jacques Cuze really was?"

The Uzzite said, "I'll admit I was stupid. I must have been to have been deceived so long. But no one need know it now that Dannto is dead. And you'll tell no one. Not as long as you're in H. And Halla here will never see anyone—except me."

Leif swallowed. Candleman could safely pretend she'd been killed during the raid and have her kept imprisoned in a secret place.

He said, "What do you know?"

The Uzzite's face did not lose any of its frozenness, but a hint of triumph crept into his voice.

"If I'd studied the French language, I'd have understood at once. But how was I to know? In this day of vast knowledge, a man can know only a small fraction of his own speciality, let alone a tongue dead for centuries. Thus, when I first heard this name Jacques Cuze uttered by a CWC prisoner, I thought it actually must be the name of a Frenchman, one who lived in the Parisian underground, and the frequency of the initials J. C. scratched here and there over the city convinced me.

"You know the inquiries I made about the initials, how I asked a linguistics man about them. His answers threw me off the track. I see now he must have been a Marcher. I ordered him arrested just before the raid tonight. But enough of that. You know how I tried to connect the first two letters of the Greek word for fish, IX, with J. C. I thought that perhaps IX stood for Ioannos Chusis or John Stream. That was a real stretch of meaning, caused by my eagerness. I didn't know then that there were two African underground churches here: the Holy Timbuktu, which uses the fish for its symbol, and the

Primitives, which use J.C. to stand both for their reputed Founder's name and for the real founder, Jikiza Chandu."

Leif looked around, desperate for anything that would give him hope of escape. There was nothing, as he'd known there would be. The Bantu's feet moved a trifle, perhaps in a death tremor.

Again Candleman tried his wristbox and had no success. He lifted Halla's head to look at her; she spat in his face. Grim-lipped, he turned away and began talking to Leif. It was as if he had to prove that Leif was the stupid one.

"I was suspicious of you for some time," he said. "You wore the lamech, true, but in these degenerate days that badge has been dishonored. There was a day when only a strict conformist to the ideals of the Sturch could pass the Elohimeter. But today the heirarchy uses that device to maintain a ruling class. Lamechian fathers, if you'll check up on it, quite often have lamechian sons. There are too many to be a coincidence.

"Moreover, I thought Halla had surely been killed in that crash. When you told me she was only slightly injured, I almost broke down."

"Nobody would have known it," said Leif. He glanced at the Man In The Dark. The feet were definitely moving.

"I have superb control," said Candleman. "I was raised as an undeviating disciple of Sigmen, real be his name. Emotion is an abhorred thing."

He paused, breathed deeply, and said, "I suspected you, especially when the case of the two Ingolfs came up. While I believe in the reality of time travel, of course, this was straining my credulity. Nevertheless, it was possible.

"As for Trausti and Palsson, I questioned them, but they must have been overwhelmed by your lamech. They saw the mangled body of Halla. Yet, because you had said she wasn't badly hurt, they deliberately denied the evidence of their eyes."

"Typical Jackasses," sneered Leif. "What else do you expect in a state where authority is the last word, and authority changes its mind from moment to moment."

"You revile us now. When you come out of H, you'll be as firm a believer as anyone."

Leif shuddered and wondered if he were going to be sick. But he kept down the urge, for he saw the Bantu sit up. Perhaps, he would . . . no . . . the man was too far gone to put up a fight.

"Jacques Cuze was haunting me day and night," continued the Uzzite. "He was in my mind while I was awake, and when I slept he walked my dreams. But I could not help thinking that there was something about him I was missing, some small clue that would enable me to catch him and his whole organization.

"Things went on in this way until I came back from Canada. I determined to drive deep in the foundation, not to rest until I found out all I could. So for a day and a night, I buried myself in the Library of Paris. I read a résumé of the history of France. I took a French dictionary, and, after learning the pronunication of French, I looked for cuze and couze. I thought perhaps the name was an adopted one, symbolizing something. But there was no such word listed.

"I looked up the many meanings of Jacques. None were appropriate. I decided I was on the wrong trail. I was lost. The man was driving me crazy, and I did not like that, for I want to be unaffected by anything or anybody."

"Even by Halla?" said Leif.

"Keep your filthy mouth closed! Listen to me! You shall learn that you Marchers, no matter how clever you are, cannot escape us. Your unreal thinking dooms you to failure!

"I sat down and thought. I said to myself that surely there must be some pattern in the general picture which I should be able to tie up with the man and his activities, something that would betray him. I tried to wrench myself from the frame of events, to stand off and see objectively as I'd never done before. I asked myself, 'What is the greatest trouble the Union is having today?' I thought that if we were deeply concerned with something, it was likely the CWC agents would be behind it. So, the answer came. We are having the most trouble in keeping our technology and production at a high level. So many techs, doctors, scientists and administrators are going to H that we have difficulty keeping the Union together. Moreover, many bright young men refuse to go into the professional schools because of the great responsiblity and the vulnerability to accusation. I saw this, yet I didn't see the answer.

"In desperation, I imported another linguistics specialist and asked him if he could make anything at all out of the name. By then I'd captured Jim Crew. The similarity of his initials didn't escape me; I wanted to know if he could be Jacques under another name. However, I found that Crew was merely the way he spelled the name of his tribe, the Kru, plus the fact that it indicated their way of living in a group and working together.

"And, of course, I got out of him that you operated willingly upon his daughter. When I learned that, I sent men to the hospital at once, but they were an hour late. And, immediately after, Dannto informed me that Halla was missing.

"Everything broke at once, for while I was giving orders to start the manhunt, the linguistics expert arrived in Paris.

"He was a specialist in the French tongue, the only one in the Union. Curiously enough, he'd been living in Haiti, because there was an isolated mountain village there where they still spoke a degenerate form of his subject. I had to locate him and have him flown here."

If Leif hadn't felt so sick from his head wound, he'd have laughed. He watched the man stride back and forth, a ridiculous figure with powderburns blacking his face, coat hanging by shreds, and his trousers reduced to a mere loincloth. Yet, he was frightening. His stiff-faced drive and single-mindedness made him a juggernaut.

Leif noticed that, though the Man In The Dark was sitting up, his head hung down and salva dripped from his lips. The wound in his shoulder oozed steadily.

Though Candleman had noticed him, he was ignoring him.

"He listened to my problem and asked me to pronounce the name. I did so. He dared to laugh, and then he told me the simple secret."

For the first time, Candleman showed signs of emotion. His hard lips curled; his voice rose.

"There it was. The whole situation in one word, or, rather, in two. There was the reason why our techs were going to such great numbers to H that we couldn't handle them. That was why our industries and sciences were lagging in production!"

Thank God, thought Leif, he still hasn't caught on to the fact that the day of Timestop was an artificial issue forced by the CWC agents! That will be the downfall of the Jacks. When a dozen rival Sigmens pop up on that day, each claiming to be the true one, civil war will rage. That, plus the breakdowns originated by Jacques Cuze, will bring the Sturch crashing into ruins.—Or so he hoped.

Candleman screeched, "You thought you were

getting away with something, didn't you, Barker? You were snickering up your sleeve all the time and conducting operations under our noses! And all the time escaping detection because of a miserable pun! By Sigmen, I should have known it was you! If only I'd called in that specialist sooner! Why, the moment he told me the truth, I saw the whole thing, and I knew who was behind it!''

He stood before the manacled man and leveled his finger at him and yelled, *"J'accuse! J'accuse!* That was the technique you Marchers used to undermine and to cripple us—the accusation technique.''

Leif gave a short laugh and said, "Yes. In your country all you have to do to condemn a man is send an anonymous accusation to the police. That's all.''

Candleman gestured wildly with his automatic.

"You've laughed too much, Marcher! By the time we're through with you at H, you'll never laugh again. You'll think it's blasphemy to be happy as long as the Sturch doesn't reign supreme. You'll no longer laugh behind our backs. You'll cringe every time you hear the name of Jacques Cuze!''

The Bantu groaned. The Uzzite's shouting seemed to have brought him halfway to life.

Candleman whirled, walked over and kicked the man in the foot. "Dirty Primitive! There'll be no more of your kind skulking under the streets and creeping out to corrupt our minds!''

Leif, watching the sitting man, saw his body shimmer and begin to change into something unpleasant. Evidently the cycle between the Bantu and the Jack was not quite a closed one. There was a line through to Leif, or else there was a splash of energy touching him. Whatever it was, he had to turn his head for a moment to steady himself. He found himself, however, unable to keep it twisted away. Even if the glimpse were revolting, it was too fascinating.

During that second of "hooking" into the cycle

between the two, Leif had undergone what Candleman was undergoing. Now, when he did gaze again, he saw the shimmer gone, replaced by the steady lines of the physical man. The vision had gone. Nor was that surprising, for the fellow had concentrated all his force upon Candleman. There was no more splash.

The Uzzite had dropped his automatic and stepped back to the wall. There he spread out his arms on each side as if groping for something solid in a dissolving world. His legs straddled an invisible horse, and his always bent-forward body was for the first time strained backwards in an agony. The face was shedding the old skin of control and was growing into knots of impossible shapes.

Leif was shaking. He had peered through a crack into hell. He was sure that if he had continued to be part of the cycle, he, too would have suffered.

Candleman had stiffened all his members. Blood had congested his skin and was driving into his protuberances with terrible pressure. The buried repressions, urges, impluses, inhibitions and thought kept all his long life inside the cell of himself were striving to leave at once. They could not do it because there was not room enough, and as fast as they did throng out, the Man In The Dark caught them and magnified them and flung them back.

And Candleman, not knowing how to discharge them, seldom having wept or laughed or sung or loved or even given reasonable vent to hate, always having clenched his fist around the value, now poured out the accumulated pressure and rottenness of a lifetime.

Eyes, ears, nose, mouth, sweat pores, every avenue of exit in his body ran with poison boiling to get out.

Leif watched him until he could bear it no longer. Rising, he picked up the fallen automatic, and he shot Candleman through the head. Nor did he doubt that the man would have thanked him for that.

A short time later, he'd taken the key from the corpse's only remaining pocket and unlocked Halla's manacles. She, in turn, freed him. Together, they helped each other down the tunnel, wounded, yet knowing the ship waited for them.

A solitary figure crouched behind them. He had refused to go with them. He was dying, and he clung to the long damp labyrinth and the lack of light. He crouched by the dead man and contemplated his work.

He would always be The Man In The Dark.

Chapter 25

THEY WALKED SEVERAL miles more and met nothing but two rats that scuttled into a hole. When they arrived at the spot that had been indicated by Beatrice, they tapped the signal upon a small red brick sticking from the wall. Presently a section swung back far enough for them to slip in sidewise. A tall, thin, brown-skinned man wearing a turban greeted them with a gun and a demand for the password. They gave it; he lowered his weapon. He was Socha Yarni, a Malay, native of Calcutta, and his job was to pilot the spaceship beneath the waters of the Seine and the Atlantic, ferrying men and materials.

As the craft was small, Leif and Halla were forced to squat upon a rug on the floor, their backs against the eternalloy wall. Bodies jammed against them, for twenty Timbuktu men and a Primitive group from another colony under Paris' west end had also taken flight. Leif was surprised to see the former, as he had not known cooperation was so close between the two nations. Dr. Djouba, huddled near him, informed him that, though the churches differed widely in beliefs, they had an agreement to use the same means of getting into the city. Aside from that, they seldom mingled.

Leif and Halla were silent for a long while. The tension of their slow trip, the many halts, the sickening odors of human bodies packed closely in a poorly ventilated space, and, above all, the terrible tiredness left in them after the chase and battle, combined to make them ill at ease, irritated, and, though it was contrary to their disposition, sullen.

Halla put her head upon his shoulder and whispered, "I'm beginning to think you've regretted what you've done."

He mastered the impulse to snap at her, but she was too sensitive to miss the roughness beneath the pretended gentleness.

"I thought the world was well lost for you," he replied.

The next instant, he knew he shouldn't have said that, for he felt tears soaking his chest. He hugged her to him and said, "'I'm sorry; I didn't mean it the way it sounded. What I meant was that I couldn't have done anything but what I did. Any other course would have made me lose you, and I just couldn't stand that. It's funny, too, for I never thought one woman could mean so much to me."

She sniffled and murmured, "Oh, I'm glad, Leif, glad you said that. Yet, because of me, you've become an exile and you'll be called a traitor. What about your parents, your friends?"

"Let me explain myself," he said. "And then there'll be no more talk about this. It'll be settled. From then on I won't have any regrets, sorrows, or self-pity coming from either you or me. I hate all three of these sentiments. They destroy you, eat you up. Have you got that through your head?"

She didn't raise her head from his breast to look at him, but he felt it nod.

"Good. Now—my parents are dead, and my close friends are none. I've been gone twelve years from March. Twelve years sacrificed for my nation. No, not for my country, for humanity. Because I don't believe in boundaries, and I hope that after this cold war is won, the lines that mark off man from man will melt away. I doubt it, though.

"During those years, the only countrymen I've known will have been Zack Roe and Ava. The others have been fleeting shadows, faces and voices and hands that I met but once or twice. Ava was the only one I could call a friend, and our relationship was peculiar. For one thing, after our first year of living as supposed man and wife, I fell into the habit of thinking of him as her. Occasionally he did something that jarred me, and I would sharply remind myself that *he* wasn't a *she*. And I surmise that during the last five years Ava began thinking of himself as female, too. I imagine that it was for that very reason he was so generally truculent with me. He *had* to assert his masculinity or lose it. He'd been somewhat feminine to begin with; that was why he could so well carry out his disguise. But he was in danger of losing his true identity, and I . . . well, I was always teasing him about his costume because I wanted to remind him of what he really was."

"Why'd he have to be a woman?"

"All because of the rigid morals of General Itskowitz of the Cold War Corps. He thought it was necessary that the hospital be controlled by both a man and a woman. The woman would oversee the nurses and the sick females and those bearing children. We could pick up a surprising amount of information and contacts from these. The logical candidate for the head nurse would be one of our women spies, but the good General didn't think so. It seemed to him that two people living as close as we would be doing would be bound to overlook the conventions and begin acting like man and wife. That'd never do. And since he couldn't induce me to marry anybody, he sent Ava as my spouse.

"When you think about it, you see how absurd his attitude was. Is it any more immoral to command a man to make love to a woman than it is to order him to kill a man?"

Halla didn't reply to that. She said, instead, "I'll bet Ava suffered."

"He did. In the first place, he was a very devout man. It hurt him to eat the food of the Jacks. In the second place, he was married, and he did not get to see his wife for all those years. Six more months, and he would have gone home, for Timestop was due to arrive. When that came, he was scheduled to leave the Haijac. His work would have been done. He'd have been greatly rewarded when he got back to March.

"Moreover, it irked him to see me making love to various women. He was as virile as any man, but he had to restrain himself because of his moral laws and also because of the part he was playing. It made him even madder that most of the lovemaking was done on the orders of the CWC. I was to influence this man and that man through his wife or sister or mistress. Most deplorable. Yet, curiously enough, it was done at the command of the aforesaid and rigidly narrow General Itskowitz. As long as it was enemy women, fine. But not with one of my own countrywomen. No, sir! I was surprised, I'll have to admit, when Ava said he'd stand off the Uzzites in the tunnel and give us a chance to go ahead. It didn't seem like him. You'd think he'd cling fiercely to the last gasp. It was possible he'd get back to March and his wife and child."

Her voice was muffled because her mouth was next to his shirt. She said, "I know he did it because of me."

"You?"

"Yes. He was a man, as I sensed from the very first. I could tell the difference in his emanations."

She touched the two rudimentary antennae beneath her mass of red hair.

"He was a man. He could not help falling in love with me. Or, at least, feeling passion."

He straightened, then forced himself to relax. "When was this?"

"When you were with Jim Crew, operating on Anadi, and we were waiting to go to Canada. It was then, you know, that he told me my sister was dead. I didn't tell you why he disobeyed Roe's orders not to inform me of that. He did it for revenge, a desire to hurt me."

"You see, he tried to make love to me, and I wouldn't let him. He was, in his way, as crazed about me as Candleman had been about my sister. He babbled that he had suffered too long, that he wouldn't stand it, that I was the most beautiful woman he'd ever seen, that he couldn't help himself, and that it wouldn't hurt us. I don't think he knew what he was saying. It was not *he* that was talking, it was his poor, frustrated body.

"I said I'd have nothing to do with him. And he turned on me, and where he had been pleading, he raged, he threatened. Finally, he told me my sister was dead. I cried. To quiet me, he gave me a grief-runner drug and allowed me to discharge my sorrow. But he hated me. Still, I know that it was because of me he sacrificed himself. I think, once he'd broken his own code, he could not go on living. His act was one of atonement. Poor fellow!"

"Yes," he said, stroking her hair, "and poor girl, too. You seem to inspire passion in every man who sees you. I'll have to watch and guard you ever minute."

"You won't have to watch me, Leif. I'm honest, and I love you."

"I'm not worried. I have you, and that's enough. You're my wife—or will be—my country, my people. I don't want any more."

Halla kept her face buried against his chest and did not say anything for a moment. He could tell she was too happy to speak. Softly, because he knew they were quite sensitive, he stroked the little bumps of her vestigial antennac. Finally, when he thought that perhaps she was falling asleep, she said, "And the Haijac Union? What about it?"

"I'll explain. You see, Halla, we have known for a long time that only the extreme efficacy of the weapons which all nations have, with the exception of Bantuland, has kept us from a hot war. So, all have resorted to a cold war with the Haijac Union against the others. But the main cold war has been between the Jacks and the Marchers and Israelis. So far the Union has been half-successful in their war against the Israeli Republics. Both have hoped their CWC's could aggravate natural weaknesses existing in the other and so accelerate them that when the time came for all-out battle, the other would go down quickly.

"The Israeli weakness is dissension between the conservative and liberal states. The Jacks know that, and their agents, I think, have been working to make even more dissension. At this moment, the Republics are on the verge of canceling the centuries-old constitution of confederation and becoming totally independent states. In fact, Sephardia and Khem have already done that.

"However, the anti-Haijacs have an advantage. We know and admit our faults, but the Union refuses to recognize it has any. That's good. For us. Because we utilized their blind suspicion and uncompromising adherence to the Sturch's principles to make them conquer themselves. You know I invented the technique: Jacques Cuze.

"Furthermore, their fanatical belief in their pseudo-scientific cosmology will bounce back and hit them in their faces. You know that when they detect unrest in the people they gandy-goose interest in Timestop, the Day of Reward. After the public's mind is taken off its troubles, the hierarchy eases the pressure and lets things go back to normal. But that can be done only so long. Then the accumulated disappointment of the mob will backfire. Provided, that is, it is given weapons to use.

"That is what will happen. We CWC-ers did not allow the last Timestop furor to die down. We kept provoking incidents. We fed inciting literature, via the comics, to the people. We've whipped up such a frenzy that the Sturch has had to go along. It's a contagious fever that's so strong even some of the hierarchy are swallowing their own medicine. And soon you'll see Timestop officially announced. Many hierarchs will try to stop it, of course, but once it's done, they can't halt it. Timestop will get nearer. The men on the top level will get more frantic. Some will lose their heads and arrest the lamechians who started the business. But when they do that, they'll discredit themselves. They'll be demonstrating that lamech-wearers aren't perfect.

"There'll be dissension and paralysis in the Allthing, the governing council. The Struch will split. Many sincere men will follow the lead of our agents. Then, Timestop arrives. A dozen men will appear, claiming to be Isaac Sigmen sailing in from his last voyage on the stream of time. These, of course, will be CWC agents. Some of these men will die, martyrs to the cause. But they'll be commemorated as heroes in March.

"The Metatrons and Sandalphons of the various states of the Union will disagree. Secession will result, and the Union will break.

"But we hope to avoid war, because it might be disastrous, and because it might be the very thing to re-unite the Jacks. If possible, we'll remain at peace and allow them to disintegrate under their own weaknesses. Moth and rust will corrupt, for the Sturch has laid up no treasures in heaven.

"It's funny, but time *will* come to stop for the Haijac; it will go static. And anything that remains static, rots. So, it may take a century, but the Sturch will die. We. through various means, will feed our democratic ideas to them. By then we, of course, may be much changed ourselves. I think the Primitives are going to influence us very much. It may be we'll find our own ideals are rather inadequate, and we'll profit from Africa and what it has to offer."

There was a lull as Leif paused for breath. During that moment, the Malay pilot, reassuring a passenger, said, loudly and distinctly, "Miss, don't worry. We get stuck in the mud every once in a while but somehow we keep going forward."